PITCH

SAVING ABBIE BOOK 1

MAGGIE ALABASTER

JO BRADLEY

Cover by Book Brander

Edited by Lily Luchesi

Proofread by Nora Hogan

Nothing Under My Feet
    Written by Abbie Hart

The ground is broken,
    the air is shattered,
    my world is nothing but an echo.
    You stole my heart and ripped it out.
    Now there's nothing under my feet.

I'm falling hard,
    you're not there to catch me.
    You watched me tumble to my knees,
    you broke me down,
    you tore my last breath.

Now there's nothing under my feet.
    Nothing to stop me.
    Nowhere to hide.
    Nothing under my feet.

I landed hard,
    but I got up.
    I won't let you take my everything away.
    I'll walk away from you,
    stronger than before.
    I have everything under my feet.

ABBIE

"HEY. You look like you could use some company." He slipped into the chair beside me before I could respond.

I turned my face to tell him to fuck off, but the words died unsaid on my lips.

He was hot as hell.

I mean the kind of hot that makes a woman melt immediately and leave a puddle on the chair.

And he knew it.

I didn't need my arrogant fuckboi radar to tell me one when I saw him. Unfortunately for me, I had a type.

Fortunately for him, he was it. Guys who were in for a couple of hours of fun before disappearing like a ghost.

Perfect. Life was too fucking short and unpredictable for commitment. Call me a cynic or a realist, I don't give a shit.

I swivelled around on my stool and rested my elbow on the table. It was too dark in this corner of the club to see the colour of his eyes, but I saw the lust in them.

I'd be blind not to.

"Hey, you might be right." I sipped my vodka and lemonade and toasted him with the glass. "What brings you to a shithole like this?"

He leaned in and smiled, flashing perfect white teeth. "You, of course. I've been looking all night for you."

"Really?" He was so full of shit, but I kinda liked it. I cocked my head at him and pouted playfully. "You haven't been looking all your life?"

Two could play the bullshit game.

He snapped his fingers. "Shit, you're right. I have. And now I've found you."

"So you have," I drawled. "What are you going to do with me?"

He pursed his lips speculatively. "That depends. What do you *want* me to do with you?"

We could start with 'everything' and go from there, but that wasn't very specific.

My heart raced like a motherfucking freight train and my panties were definitely wet. At this point, I didn't care what he did with me, as long as he did *something*.

"Hmmm." I licked my lips slowly and watched him watch my tongue slide across my mouth. "You look like you know what to do with your hands."

He had big hands with long, firm fingers. No rings but plenty of tattoos. He had a full sleeve on one arm and almost as many on the other. I bet there were plenty more under his tight-fitting black T-shirt. Even in the dim light, I could tell he was ripped. His biceps fought to escape the fabric.

I bet his body was harder than concrete. Harder than stone.

Not just his body either, there was something hard about his face, his eyes, like he knew how to handle himself.

He smiled and one eyebrow quirked upward slightly.

"As it happens, I do," he said slowly. He didn't even look to check if anyone was watching before he slipped a hand up my skirt.

It was too dark for anyone to see much anyway, but I had enough vodka that I didn't care if they did.

He slid his hand up my leg to the gusset of my

panties. There, he started to trace slow circles around the lacy black fabric.

My hand tightened on the glass. A jolt of heat went all the way through me, from my head to my curling toes.

He peeled the gusset aside and grazed his fingers across the front of my pussy.

Oh. My. God.

Without thinking, I adjusted my position on the stool to spread my thighs wider, giving him more access to my suddenly ravenous pussy.

He smiled and circled my clit with his fingertips a few times before he slid a finger inside me, deep enough to make me hungrier still.

I bit back a moan. The music in the club was loud, but not so loud I could scream and not be heard.

"Holy shit, you're so wet." He shifted his own position, twisting his hips closer to me before slipping another finger inside me. Then another. He curled his fingers to caress my g-spot, while the heel of his hand rubbed over my clit.

He was better than good with his hands. He fed my needs with practiced skill that left me panting with ragged breaths.

I half opened my eyes and glanced around, but no

one was looking our way. No one would see me tip my head back, or roll my hips as I drew closer to the edge.

I bit my lip and panted through my nose, suppressing the moan that slipped out of my mouth as I came.

I bucked harder against his hand, milking the sensation for every delicious, orgasmic drop. Stars exploded across my vision. Blood raced through my ears, louder than the music which thudded through speakers in the ceiling.

Heat thundered through me for at least a minute, maybe two, before I finally came down in a quivering, whimpering puddle.

"Fuck," I said, too softly to be heard. Judging by the grin on his face, he read my lips well enough.

He slid his fingers out of me and stuck them in his mouth.

"Tasty." He grinned around his fingers and sucked them for a moment longer.

Shit, that was hot.

"You're incredible with your hands." I should probably not feed what was clearly a healthy ego already, but I had to give credit where it was due.

"You look like you're good with your mouth." He gave me another speculative look.

The suggestion might have pissed another woman off, but I smiled. He was right about that; I was.

I fixed my panties and skirt and slid down into the perfect darkness under the table.

He said something that might have been, "Holy fuck," as I unfastened the front of his jeans.

I pushed them down enough to let his thick erection spring free. I slid my hand up and down his blazing hot length, from his head to his balls, making him harder still.

Slowly, teasingly, I ran the tip of my tongue over the tip of his cock. I savoured the taste of his precum before I took the rest of him in my mouth.

He reached down to tangle his hand in my blond hair, holding me in place while I sucked hard.

I massaged his balls with my fingers until he was quivering. His hips moved, thrusting him deeper into my mouth. I took as much of him as I could.

Not wanting to hurry, I slipped my mouth off him and ran my tongue up and down his length and around his head.

His fingers tightened on my hair, almost to the point of pain. I wouldn't have minded if he hurt me a little, but I wasn't in a position to communicate that right now.

I slipped my mouth back over him and sucked harder and faster. He bucked, driving himself deeper and deeper into my throat. I grazed my nails lightly over his balls, marvelling at the heat of his skin.

He stilled and a shudder went through him.

Hot cum squirted from his tip, into my throat. I slid my mouth off his cock and swirled his juices around like it was fine wine. Instead of spitting, I slid over so the dim light could hit my face. I looked directly at him and swallowed.

I read his lips this time when he said, "Holy fuck."

He let go of my hair and helped me out from under the table, and back into my stool.

"You aren't what I expected when I walked up to you." He kept my hand in his.

"Oh? Would you have walked up to me if you knew how it would go?" I cocked my head at him.

He grinned. "I wouldn't have waited an hour to talk to you. I would have approached you the moment I laid eyes on you."

Sure he waited that long. He didn't strike me as the shy type. I resisted the urge to roll my eyes. A little bit of flattery, even if it was bullshit, was good for my ego. Honestly, I could use the boost.

"You should have. I was sitting here all by myself." Watching and waiting for someone like him to come up or catch my eye. I hadn't seen him before he sat down beside me. He probably just walked in the door. Whatever, we had fun and weren't going to see each other after tonight. A few white lies and harmless flirtation wouldn't hurt.

"A woman like you wouldn't have sat here by herself for too long," he said smoothly. "It's a miracle someone didn't beat me to it. It must be my lucky day."

"Not just lucky," I said. "I don't let any old guy stick his hand up my skirt."

I liked sex, and lots of it, but I had *some* standards.

"Of course you don't," he said like he actually knew me. "I'm surprised a girl like you would even talk to a guy like me."

I rolled my eyes playfully. As if he didn't know exactly how hot he was. He probably had women panting after him wherever he went. If there were any surprises to be had here, it's that he was talking to me, not surrounded by a crowd of horny girls, all prettier and slimmer than me.

"Like I said, I was sitting here alone." A smile tugged at the corners of my mouth.

He laughed. "Ouch." He stroked his thumb over the back of my hand. "Do you live near here?"

"I'm staying in a hotel close by." I didn't elaborate.

I doubted he'd be interested that I was in Sydney for work. We didn't even have the kind of relationship that ran to sharing names, much less details like that.

"Do you want me to walk you back there?" he asked. "It's not safe for a woman by herself around here."

I tilted my chin up. "I can take care of myself, but sure. I could use the company."

I wasn't naïve. I knew he was hoping for round two. So was I. And round three after that. He looked like he had enough stamina to spare. I certainly did.

"Great. Have you finished your drink?" He nodded towards the glass on the table.

I looked at it sideways and grimaced. The ice melted. The vodka and lemonade would taste like water. Still, because I didn't like waste, I picked it up and threw the rest of it back.

"Now I have." I placed the glass back on the table and slid off my stool.

"You're wild." He held out his hand. "I like that in a woman."

"That's me." I took his hand and let him curl his fingers around mine as we walked to the door.

A couple of guys sitting at a table near ours glanced at us as we walked past. They grinned.

Apparently what we did hadn't gone unnoticed after all.

I grinned back and gave them both an air kiss. I should try to be more discreet next time in case I was recognised. Whatever. Let them talk.

Could it damage my reputation any more than it already was? It was pretty fucking tarnished.

Yeah, there was still room to make it worse.

We slipped out into the steamy air of a Sydney summer night. Or was it morning by now?

"It's just down that way." I gestured. The nicer hotels were in the opposite direction. Right now, I couldn't afford to stay there. The cheap fleabag place I was in was enough of a stretch. With any luck, my meeting tomorrow would change all of that.

It had to, I was ready to be back on top.

He didn't look like he was judging me. He could get stuffed if he was. I would have let go of his hand and walked by myself. I liked his company, but I didn't need his approval.

"What's your—"

Whatever he was about to say, was interrupted by a man stepping out of a side alley.

He was dressed from head to toe in black, from his ripped jeans to the hoodie that obscured most of his face.

I took in all of that before I noticed one hand deep in the pocket in the front of his hoodie.

Shit.

He pulled out his hand, and with it, a dark-coloured pistol. The kind you see in the movies, usually in the hands of secret agents or bad guys.

Slowly, he raised the gun.

I knew nothing about guns, except the end the bullets came out of was pointed at us.

My bet was, he wasn't a secret agent.

Fuck.

I froze.

2

ABBIE

"LONG TIME NO SEE, ZEKE," the gunman said.

What the fuck?

Zeke grabbed my arm and shoved me behind him.

"Accosting innocent people on the street now, Jonah?" Zeke asked lightly. "That's a new low, even for you."

I eyed the hand that held the gun. He looked like he knew how to use it. The fact he knew Zeke was no consolation whatsoever. What the crap had he dragged me into? Was this some kind of set up? I was going to be pissed if it was. If it wasn't, how could Zeke sound so calm? I was about ready to pee my panties.

Jonah shrugged one shoulder. His hand didn't

even waver. "Just doing what the boss wants me to do. He has a message for you."

Zeke's grip tightened on my arm. "Save it. I don't want to hear Reuben's bullshit."

Jonah aimed the gun at Zeke's head. "Nevertheless, I'm going to say what I was sent here to say."

"There's no message you can give me that I haven't heard a million times before." It sounded like Zeke's patience was running out.

Honestly, it wasn't *his* patience I was worried about, it was the guy holding the motherfucking firearm. I had no reason to assume it wasn't locked and loaded.

"Maybe you should listen," I suggested. "I mean, whatever it takes for us all to walk away from this." Just when I thought life couldn't get any worse, it did. This was all kinds of messed up. I should have stayed in my shitty hotel room and watched reruns of some old sitcom on the tiny TV. Not even an orgasm and a blow job were worth dying for.

"You should listen to the chick," Jonah said. "Shut your mouth and open your ears for once."

Zeke bristled visibly, but fell silent. He oozed anger.

Silently, I begged him to contain it before bullets started to fly.

"The boss said your time is running out," Jonah said. "Your time and his patience. He's waited long enough while you played around. He wants you back with the family."

The breath caught in my throat. Boss? Family? What the hell was this guy into? Trust me to be attracted to someone dangerous. One of these days I would make better life choices but evidently today was not that day.

I really needed to start thinking with my brain and not my pussy.

"I'm not going back." Zeke's face was a stone wall, cold and expressionless.

"I should go and leave you two to it." I stepped back, but Zeke still held my arm.

"I could make an example out of her," Jonah said. He swivelled his upper body until the gun was aimed at my head.

The barrel looked approximately fucking huge. A bullet coming out of that would spread my brains for metres.

Holy shit, let me get out of this intact.

I tugged my arm free of Zeke and held both of my hands up. My heart raced so fast I thought it might stop dead. I've been scared before, who hasn't? But never like this.

"This has nothing to do with me," I protested. "I don't even know this guy." Just because I had his cock down my throat twenty minutes ago didn't mean I was going to die for him.

Jonah's eyes weren't on me, they were on Zeke. Apparently he didn't care if I knew him or not. This was all about trying to get Zeke to comply.

"Leave her out of it," Zeke snapped. Apparently he wasn't in a complying mood. "You've delivered your message, now fuck off. Tell Reuben I'll think about it."

"He's not gonna be satisfied with that." Jonah cocked the gun and stepped closer to me.

Shit, just when things were starting to look up, I was going to die on the street, a bullet through my skull.

Fucking wonderful. The tabloids were going to love every minute of this. I could see the headlines now.

I shook my head and took a step back. "Please—"

Sweat sprang up under my arms. Was this where I was supposed to see my life flash in front of me? All I saw was a bunch of misplaced trust and bad choices, coupled with being screwed over time and time again.

"This doesn't need to—"

Zeke threw himself at Jonah. He grabbed the arm he held the gun in and forced it down towards the ground. The gun fired, slamming a bullet towards the concrete.

I squealed and instinctively jumped back. The bullet hit hard, bounced to about the height of my knee, then clattered on the ground.

Zeke and Jonah wrestled for the gun. Just like Jonah obviously knew how to handle one, Zeke clearly knew how to fight to take one from someone else. He kept Jonah's arm at an angle where a bullet wouldn't hit his foot if it discharged again.

Unfortunately Jonah wasn't going to let the gun be taken from him that easily. In terms of size and sheer muscle, they were equally matched.

I should take the opportunity to run away. It would have been the smart thing to do. On the other hand, I had a long list of dumb choices behind me. What was another one?

Even if it might get me killed.

For some reason, I couldn't walk away and let Jonah kill Zeke. For all I knew, he'd come after me to take care of any witnesses. For self preservation alone, I had good reason to do what I did.

I stepped closer and waited for the right opportunity. Zeke jerked Jonah's arm to the side and I took my chance. I twisted my body to the side and jammed the heel of my stiletto into the top of Jonah's foot.

He shouted with rage. Zeke took the chance to grab the gun and turn it on him.

I started to exhale with relief, but almost choked on the breath.

I wasn't expecting to see the grin on Zeke's face. It was dark and cold, in spite of the upturn of his mouth. It sent shivers and jolts of heat right through me, in equal measure.

I should absolutely not find anything about this hot. What did that say about me that I did? Yeah okay, I already knew I was fucked up. This level of fucked up was slightly surprising though. Oh well, it was never too late to learn these things about yourself.

"Now whose time is running out?" Zeke asked. He actually sounded amicable for someone who was threatening another man. Even reasonable.

"I know he would have killed me." My voice shook. "But no one needs to die here. Do they?"

Jonah stood with his hands raised. He looked more pissed off than scared. "No one needs to die. But Ezequiel isn't going to kill me. Are you Zeke?"

"I'm fucking tempted," Zeke said. "Right now I'm struggling to think of a good reason why I shouldn't."

"Because murder is a bad idea," I said. Why did I get the impression neither of them thought so and both committed it in the past?

Abbie, I told myself, *you really need to learn to judge people better.*

What started out as a bit of fun had ended up a complete fucking mess. I should have told Zeke to get lost when he sat down next to me.

My still-damp panties said otherwise. I was apparently more depraved than I gave myself credit for.

"You'll also make a mess," I pointed out. "Blood and brains and all that stuff..." I took a few steps away from them. I could slip out of my stilettos and run. I was almost certain Zeke wouldn't kill a witness.

Right?

Oh God, I was so screwed.

Silence fell for a full minute before Zeke said, "Get the hell out of here, Jonah. Give Reuben my message. I'm not coming back, no matter what he does. I'm done with the family. I don't know how to make that any clearer."

"The boss is going to be pissed," Jonah said. He

shrugged, turned and disappeared back into the shadows.

Zeke exhaled loudly. "Shit." He took the clip out of the gun and shoved it into his pocket. A look of distaste on his face, he held the gun by the trigger guard, as though he suddenly found it repugnant.

"I would bet anything this was used in a violent crime in a city the same time I was there. It would be easy enough to find—" He shook his head. "I'll get rid of it."

Did I even want to know how he knew how to get rid of a gun? Okay, I kind of did. At the same time, I knew better than to ask. Whatever was going on here, I was in it deep enough already. I should get the hell out before I drowned.

"Does this sort of shit happen to you often?" I asked. Did I want to know the answer to that too? Well fuck, the words are already out of my mouth anyway.

He laughed bitterly. "More times than I'd like. Reuben is stubborn and persistent."

"Is he your boss?" I asked.

"Not my boss," he said. "It's a long story. You're better off not knowing about it. I'm sorry you got dragged into this. If I knew it was gonna happen, I would have taken you the long way round."

"You still would have approached me in the club?" I asked. "Even knowing doing that might have gotten me killed?"

He tucked the gun away somewhere under his shirt and grinned. "Hell yeah I would. I don't regret a minute of that."

His expression faltered. "I was going to offer you another round, but I need to get rid of this thing and get you somewhere safe. I can't guarantee Jonah and Reuben don't have something else up their sleeves. Like I said, Reuben is persistent."

"I'm starting to dislike this Reuben guy," I said dryly. People who didn't take no for an answer were the worst, especially if they sent gunmen after people.

Zeke laughed. "He's not the most likeable guy on the planet." He reclaimed my hand and we resumed walking towards my hotel.

"Is that why you got away from him?" I asked.

"It's one reason amongst many," he agreed. "I prefer to live my life in a very different way to what he would like."

"Is Reuben your father?" I guessed.

Zeke snorted. "Hell no. He likes to think he is. He's a pain in my ass, but I'll deal with him."

"You seem like you know how to handle yourself." I stopped outside the front of the crappy hotel I was staying in. It was almost too embarrassing to be seen there, but I felt safer with him than if I ditched him a block back.

He smiled and placed his hand on the wall behind my left shoulder. "Seems like I know how to handle you pretty well too." He leaned in for a soft but lingering kiss.

"You didn't hear me complaining." For a start, the music was too loud anyway. But no, I enjoyed every second of it. If it wasn't for that asshole and his gun, I could be enjoying a few more hours of it. Instead, all I really wanted to do was get into my room and hide under the covers. Yeah, I know, blankets are no protection from bullets. Let me have my moment.

"Me either." He gave me a soft smile. "I'm sorry our night got cut short. Next time, I'll be more prepared."

We both knew there wasn't going to be a next time. Still, it was nice to hear that if there was, I might not be accosted at the end of a gun.

I knew there was a reason I hated guns. They were really good for ruining my sex life. That seemed like a good enough reason to dislike them to me. That and the whole, 'I could be dead right now,' thing. All in all, it wasn't a positive experience.

"Thank you for an interesting time," I said.

"Interesting?" He mused. "I always strive to be interesting, but I don't think this was exactly what you had in mind. It was certainly not a part of my plans."

I shrugged as though I hadn't been absolutely terrified only a few minutes earlier.

"Whatever keeps the adrenaline pumping."

"I can think of a lot of things better than that." He brushed his lips over mine again, then stepped away. "I should hurry up. It won't be long before Jonah calls the cops and I don't want to be found with a gun on me. That involves way too many questions I don't have all the answers for."

I suspected he had all the answers, he didn't want to give them. Before I could say that, he melted away into the night.

I was left alone outside the front of the fleabag hotel, under the light of a single, flickering bulb.

3

ZEKE

I STRETCHED my legs out in front of me, leaned back and laced my hands behind my head.

No doubt I looked every bit the arrogant rock star everyone in the room expected of me.

It was a role I was happy to embrace. Would anyone expect anything less from the lead singer of Wolf Venom, the hottest band on the whole fucking planet?

"I'm sure you're wondering why I asked you to come here." Jackson Beckett crossed his arms over his chest and scanned the room. Our band's manager, he was good at throwing his weight around. We even listened to him. Sometimes.

"We might be curious," Asher DiMarco said with a shrug and indifferent smirk. The blonde drummer was at least as arrogant as me. And had as much baggage in his background.

As far as I knew, his brother never sent anyone after him with a gun, but there was a first time for everything.

I glanced past him to where Landon and Channing sat so close they were almost in each other's laps. The bass player and the band's saxophonist were inseparable.

To my knowledge, they'd never been with a woman unless they shared her with each other. They were a package deal, which seemed to work for plenty of groupies. When groupies weren't around, they could barely keep their hands off each other.

If you asked me, they were pretty fucking cute.

Much cuter than Penn, the keyboardist, who sat on the other side of them, his face a typical scowl.

Across his knuckles, the words *Fuck Life* were tattooed in black ink. That was basically his motto and approach to everything.

"You could have texted," Penn growled.

The side of Jackson's mouth twitched in annoyance, but he didn't rise to the bait Penn threw out. Not exactly.

"What I have to say needs to be done face-to-face," Jackson said coolly. "With the new album about to drop and the impending tour, the label has decided to make some changes."

"What changes?" Asher asked carefully. He eyed Jackson suspiciously.

"And by label, do you mean Levi?" I asked. He owned White Wolf Records. While other people worked under him, sometimes he liked to make sudden tweaks. And by sudden I meant heavy-handed. Whatever was going on here, it smelled of Levi Jones.

Jackson ignored my question and responded to Asher. "We'll be adding someone else to the tour."

"We already have a support act." Penn's scowl deepened. "Blazing Violet." He seemed to loathe them as much as he loathed everyone else, including himself. Okay, especially himself.

"She wouldn't be supporting you," Jackson said carefully. "More like a co-headline."

"What the fuck?" Penn set up in his chair. "No way. We don't share the stage."

I dropped my hands and sat up too. "Wait a minute. Am I being replaced?"

This went from smelling of Levi to smelling of Reuben. Getting rid of that gun was hard enough. Luckily I knew a guy, a contact from back when I worked for my brother. He owed me a couple of favours. Even then, he wasn't happy about it, but he did it anyway.

By now, the serial number and anything that might connect it to me or Reuben, or anyone else, was gone. Somebody would probably get away with murder because of it, but I had no choice.

"If Zeke is out, then I'm out," Tully said. The lead guitarist was a man of few words, but when he spoke, people listened. Particularly when he was making sense like he was right now.

Jackson raised his hands in a placating gesture. "No one is being replaced. The label signed a new singer and her reputation could use some work. Things got a little messy with her former label."

I picked up a bottle of water from the floor beside my chair and unscrewed the top.

"And by messy you mean—?"

I took a sip as the door opened and she walked inside.

I almost choked on my mouthful of water.

I recognised that blond hair, that beautiful face, her incredible figure, and of course that mouth. I almost still felt it wrapped tight around my cock. And the way her muscles contracted around my fingers when they were deep inside her. Not to mention the fact it was a public place and she didn't seem shy at all.

The memory alone was enough to make my cock strain against my jeans.

Down boy. That didn't stop my dick from throbbing.

I coughed to clear my throat and put the lid back on the bottle.

"Yeah, she's pretty fucking messy," Penn snarled.

"I see Mr Pennington is already acquainted with Abbie," Jackson said dryly.

Her eyes—they were brilliant blue—scanned the room. They opened a little wider when she saw me. His skin paled slightly.

Yeah, she might not be the only one whose face was a bit whiter.

"I'm not acquainted," Penn said. "Her last label dropped her. Why the fuck is she here?"

That was a good question. I couldn't seem to tear my eyes off her to look back at Jackson for the answer.

"Like I said," Jackson said slowly, "Abbie has signed with the label and we have work to do to rebuild her reputation."

Penn snorted. "I'll fucking say."

"I'm sorry, I must be missing something." Asher looked around at everyone, obviously confused.

Abbie slipped into a chair, chin tilted up but still clearly uncomfortable. She glanced at me.

I offered her a smile. She gave me half a one in return.

Jackson sighed. "Things were said unfairly…" He gestured towards Abbie. "Perhaps you would like to explain."

She looked like she would like to do anything *but* explain, but she sighed.

"As Jackson said, the press has been damaging to my reputation. To the point where Onyx Riot Records decided they needed to distance themselves from me."

"She was fucking the boss," Penn said. "The *married* boss."

Every eye in the room was on her. She squirmed with discomfort.

"I had a relationship with him while he and his wife weren't together. I was led to believe they were getting a divorce." She sucked in a breath. "When they reconciled, she wanted me out. And so, I was out." She looked pissed as fuck about that.

Fair enough, I would be pissed too if someone was using me like that. And then I got the blame.

"Then there was the twenty-four hour marriage," Penn said relentlessly. "Was that a publicity stunt?"

She glanced down to the floor before she looked back up again. "It was twenty-six hours. For the first two, I thought it was real."

A heavy silence followed her words.

Penn snorted. He clearly didn't believe a word of it.

Me, I wasn't sure what to believe. She seemed to live life unapologetically and that was being held against her. If that was the case, then it was bullshit.

"How come you know so much about her?" Landon asked.

"Penn likes to read about himself in the tabloids," Channing said. "He finds out about other people that way too."

Penn stuck his finger up at him, a letter F tattooed at the base of his finger. He was all class.

"As you can see," Jackson spoke loud enough to draw the attention back to him. "Abbie Hart is signed to White Wolf Records now. As you know, we take pride in taking care of our own." He ignored Penn's snort.

"So Abbie will be touring with Wolf Venom. She'll be singing between Blazing Violet and you guys. And singing a couple of songs with you." His gaze swivelled towards me.

Aware everyone was now looking at me, I shrugged one shoulder. "Sounds good to me. The more the merrier."

She looked grateful, although she must have known as well as I did we had little choice in the matter. I could have fought it and let it get ugly, but I didn't see the point. It wouldn't hurt us to share the stage with her and have her along for the ride.

If she wanted to continue what we started last night, I was more than okay with that.

Not the part where we had a gun pointed at us, but the part where I got to come down her throat. And where she looked up at me and swallowed my cum like it was ice cream.

My pulse thundered at the thought.

"This is all kinds of fucked up," Penn growled. "We don't need a woman screwing up our act."

"Your objection is noted—" Jackson started to say.

Abbie sat up in her chair, interrupting him, her hands on her hips. She glared at Penn. "What is your problem? Did I do something to you?"

He rolled his eyes at her and looked away.

"That's just Penn," I said. "He's got a chip on his

shoulder the size of Sydney Harbour. He's all right when you get to know him."

"I am not," Penn said without looking back.

I shrugged at Abbie and smiled. "The rest of us are more or less harmless."

She looked sceptical, and I was almost certain she was going to bring up Jonah, but she didn't. She had no way of knowing how much the other guys knew. I appreciated her attempt at discretion.

"Are you sure about that?" Asher grinned. "I'm not sure if the word harmless describes any of us accurately."

"That's why I said more or less." I nodded my head in his direction. "She can decide for herself where we stand on the spectrum. I suspect she's going to get to know us pretty fucking well over the next few months."

Personally, I wanted to get to know her a *lot* more intimately.

Penn scowled at her like she was something he scraped off his shoe, but the rest of the guys never turned down an opportunity for a fuck. Truthfully, Penn never turned down the opportunity either, but he seemed to have taken a violent dislike to Abbie. That was his problem, not hers, and certainly not mine. Since he pretty much hated everyone, it was normal for him anyway.

"I expect you to keep an eye on her," Jackson said. "The publicity is going to be brutal, but if anyone is up to it, you guys are."

"Hell yeah we are," I agreed.

"Are we bodyguards now?" Tully asked. I couldn't tell what he thought about the arrangement. He usually just rolled with whatever happened. "I don't think there's anything in our contracts about saving Abbie from the press."

"Like I said, we look after our own," Jackson said.

"Is she *fucking* Levi?" Penn had looked back around and was now glaring at Abbie. "Is that what this is about?"

It was a fair question, I supposed. Levi Jones was not known for keeping his cock in his pants any more than I was. Any more than any of us was.

"No," Abbie said firmly. "We've met a few times but that was it. Believe it or not, I got my contract based on *merit*." She matched Penn's look, fury for fury until her words sank in.

"Fuck off," Penn snarled. "We're all here because we're talented and worked bloody hard."

"Right," Jackson said loudly. "You're *all* here because you're talented. Abbie and Wolf Venom. If you fight like this in public, the press is going to have a field day. Don't. Give them. A fucking. Field day. I'm sure none of you wants to be dropped."

"No we don't," I said quickly. "They'll learn to get along." I gave Penn a meaningful look. He didn't need to make this harder than it was.

He shrugged and looked away.

I sighed to myself. I had a feeling getting along was going to be easier said than done.

On the other hand, the way she stuck up for herself made my cock even harder. I would have to try to find a way to get her alone.

4

ZEKE

"THIS IS BULLSHIT." Penn shoved open the door to the rehearsal room so hard it banged against the wall and bounced. He pushed it back and stepped inside ahead of me.

"Yeah, tell us what you really think," I said sarcastically. "There's no point bitching about it. It is what it is."

He gave me a look that suggested he'd barely even started bitching and stalked over to the coffee machine at the back of the room.

The Australian arm of White Wolf Records took pretty good care of us. They gave us the rehearsal space in the same building as the recording studio in Sydney. Everything was state of the art, of course. Levi spared no expense where we were concerned.

It wasn't exclusively ours, in theory, but we were here more than most of the other acts.

The coffee machine was an added bonus. We asked for a fully stocked beer fridge too, but they declined for some reason. Something to do with not getting drunk on the job.

Spoilsports.

"He'll get over it." Asher gave me a playful shove further into the room.

I grinned and shoved him back.

"Now, now, children." Tully spoke in a squeaky joking voice. "If you keep doing that, someone's going to get hurt."

Asher and I exchanged a glance before we both zeroed in on the guitarist with a series of air punches.

He put up his hands in mock self-defence and laughed. "You guys are idiots."

"We love you too." Asher stopped to sniff the air before heading down to the back of the room. "Hell yeah, coffee."

"Coffee, our real true love." I grabbed myself a mug and started to spoon instant granules into it.

"Speak for yourself," Landon said from the couch under the window. He was lying across the couch, his head in Channing's lap. Channing brushed strands of blue hair lightly off Landon's face.

Penn glanced over his shoulder at me. "Everyone is your true love," he said scathingly. "Until you zip your pants back up. I'm guessing that's behind your support of Abbie. You're hoping to get her into bed. Then what?"

I poured hot water into my mug and ignored his correct accusation. "I support not making waves when making them won't help anyone."

I put down the electric kettle and picked up the bottle of milk. "Don't tell me you didn't notice how cute she was." I gave him the side eye. There was no way he'd missed that. He was as big a fuckboi as the rest of us.

I didn't bother to explain that Abbie and I were already acquainted. That would raise questions I didn't feel like answering. At some point, if it came up, I'd deal with it, but I wasn't going to volunteer the information just yet.

"Cute is irrelevant," Penn said. "If she sucks, she's going to make us all look bad." He scowled at me like having her along was somehow my fault.

"She's not gonna suck." Asher sipped his coffee. "The label wouldn't have signed her if she was. And they wouldn't send her on tour with us either. Right, Zeke?"

"Exactly," I agreed.

Asher was wrong about one thing, she *did* suck. And she was very good at it. Thinking about her mouth made my balls hurt. Having her around might be harder than I thought.

Literally. Whatever, I'd deal with that too.

"You know," I said slowly, "I'm going to have to spend more time rehearsing with her than the rest of you will. If she and I are going to sing duets, then we're going to have to do it. A lot."

That didn't sound like the worst thing ever. I liked the idea of spending more time with her. And doing it. But at some point she was going to ask about the gun and Jonah. I'd have to decide what I was going to say to her. Something which would alleviate any fears she might have about me, while being as close to the truth as possible.

At least I could assure her having guns waved at me wasn't a frequent occurrence.

Usually.

"Your loss." Penn drank his coffee in about two mouthfuls, which was impressive because it must have been hot. No one ever claimed he was normal.

He set his cup down on the bench like he

expected someone else to wash it, and walked over to his keyboard.

Like we often did, we leaned against walls, benches and each other, and listened to him warm up.

He played the first couple of minutes of Beethoven's "Moonlight Sonata", while chills travelled up and down my spine. Some days, he could almost bring me to tears. At times, it was hard to reconcile Beau Pennington, the musician, with Penn, the keyboard player with an attitude bigger than Australia.

For such a grumpy asshole, the music he made with his fingers was nothing short of beautiful. He would say it's no big deal, but I've never heard anyone who played keyboard the way he could. The emotion he put into his music was something you couldn't learn. You either had it or you didn't. Lucky for us, he did.

His unmistakable talent was one of the reasons he was part of Wolf Venom, in spite of his attitude. His talent was also a big part of the reason for his attitude.

Us rock stars are a complicated lot.

Penn stopped playing and looked over his shoulder. "You guys gonna stand there or are we going to rehearse?"

"Technically I'm lying down." Landon grinned and sat up.

Penn eyed him and shook his head, but for once didn't say anything.

I shook off the effect of Penn's playing and grabbed the microphone.

The moment my hand curled around it, I got that thrill of excitement. The one that reminded me I'm an actual motherfucking rock star. Not just that, but I was the lead singer of Wolf Venom, the hottest, coolest band in the world. With the coolest name to match.

I turned on the mic and waited for the guys to get themselves organised.

I stood facing them, my game face on.

"Good afternoon and welcome to rehearsal," I said into the microphone. I tried to sound like the Chief Purser on a long haul flight. Why? Because sometimes I was a dork. "Thank you all for coming here today." Without an audience, the rest of the band was the crowd. "Keep your seatbelt fastened and prepare for a shit load of turbulence." Okay, that was off script, but it got the desired response.

The guys chuckled.

"You should have been a clown," Tully teased.

I raised the mic to my lips. "Who says I'm not? I make you guys laugh."

"We're easily pleased," Asher said from behind his drums. He played *ba-dum-tish* and grinned.

"Yeah," Channing agreed. "Our bar is really low." He played a few lively notes on his saxophone.

"You know how to hurt a guy." Without waiting for further insults to be flung my way, I launched into the first song of our new set list.

"Take Me Down Lower" could be interpreted any number of ways. The lyrics worked for people in a toxic relationship, or they could relate to oral sex. I guessed it depended on your circumstances and how dirty your mind was.

Personally, I loved songs that let the listener decide what they were about. They were always the ones we got asked about the most. Especially the ones laced with the kind of innuendos that went over kids heads, but adult listeners understood and adored.

Everyone liked to assume we put some hard and fast meaning to everything, so to speak. Sometimes we did, often we didn't.

Very often, we gave a different explanation whenever we were asked. Usually more outrageous than the last one. I think the latest had something to do with a submarine.

Who knows if anyone bought that, but it was good for a laugh.

I smiled as the guys scrambled to catch up.

Thank fuck they did. They could have left me to sing by myself. That would serve me right for being a smart ass. The guys didn't usually leave me hanging though, and certainly not when it mattered.

I strutted around the rehearsal room like I was on stage. Wishing I was.

By the end of the song, we'd all fallen into our usual easy rhythm. These tracks were new, but we played them a crap load of times already. Enough to have them down pat in our sleep.

I paused for the bridge and lowered the mic. For a good ten seconds or so, I was able to appreciate the other guy's playing. If you asked me, I would say we were pretty fucking good.

I wasn't sure how Abbie would fit into the set, but we would make it work. And then, if I could fit into her, that would be even better.

Just thinking about her and her mouth, I almost forgot to bring the microphone back up and keep singing.

That wouldn't have gone unnoticed by the other

guys. Especially Penn. The guy got pissy if any of us screwed up that badly.

Yeah, okay, when was he not pissy? He was a perfectionist. There was nothing wrong with that. I sure as hell didn't want to look like an idiot, especially in front of an audience.

Particularly an audience full of people with their phones in their hands, recording me making a fool of myself.

That kind of thing was difficult to get past.

We finished the first song and fell silent. Closer to the tour, we would play the full set all the way through, multiple times. At this point, we would stop and discuss any tweaks we needed to make.

"Are we throwing in some covers?" Penn asked, like he'd hate the answer, no matter what it was. "Or are we supposed to sing her songs?"

"There's a third option in there," Tully pointed out. "A few people know one or two of our songs. It's possible she might too."

Landon snorted. "Only one or two?"

"Maybe three," Tully acknowledged.

Since our last three albums went multi-platinum, it was definitely more than that, but we got his point.

"There's no reason why Abbie can't learn a couple

of our songs," I said. "I'll be happy to teach her if she doesn't."

"Are you sure she isn't after your job?" Asher asked teasingly. "That might be where it starts."

I smirked at him. "No one is taking my job."

No one was going to replace Zeke Brantley, not now, not ever. My distinct vocals were the reason Wolf Venom stood out from the rest of the pack. Why we were so popular.

Asher grinned. "That's what they all say, right before they lose their job."

I flipped him off and said, "You mean how we could replace you with a drum machine?"

"Ouch." He laughed. "A drum machine can't do what I can."

"What is that?" Tully asked.

"Look hot while playing the drums." Asher did a short roll and hit a cymbal, grooving while he did it and finishing with a flourish.

"He's got you there," Landon said.

"Thank you." Asher bowed over his drums. "I live to please."

"Don't we all," I said into the microphone. That brought my mind back to Abbie.

After we left Jackson's office, she'd stayed behind to talk to him about a few things.

I was ninety-nine percent sure Penn thought he was fucking her, but I doubted it. Jackson was more professional than that. Anyway, if he was going to sleep with any of the talent, it probably wouldn't be in his office.

Maybe.

Hell, I might be way off there. I just...didn't want to think of him and her together.

Strangely enough, her and any of the other guys wouldn't bother me, but our manager was like a father to us, in a way. Them sleeping together would be weird. But their business, of course, if they chose to do that.

"I'll talk to Jackson about it," I said. "And Abbie. Rest assured you'll all know long before the tour starts. We'll have plenty of time to rehearse and make any adjustments we think need to be made."

"The only adjustment we need to make is no adjustment," Penn said. He turned his attention back to his keyboard.

I lowered the mic so my sigh wouldn't echo through the room.

It was going to be a long tour if Penn was going to hate on Abbie the entire time.

5

ABBIE

"This is the rehearsal room. Zeke will take good care of you."

For some reason, Jackson seemed relieved to leave me with the guys. We'd had an amicable conversation, but I suspected he thought my reputation would be insurmountable. Or at least, a lot of work.

Imagine how I must feel.

He opened the door just as the guys finished a song.

They all turned towards me. Some of their expressions warm, others hostile. Landon and Channing looked curious.

Thankfully one of the warmer faces was Zeke's.

"Hey," he said into the mic just because he could.

I would have been able to hear him without it. Some of us liked to hear our own voices through speakers. I was guilty of that myself.

Zeke looked even hotter here than he did at the club. It might be the light and it might be because he looked comfortable with the microphone in his hand.

I cleared my throat.

"Hello." Even without the other night between us, it was hard to tear my eyes off Zeke.

He had a magnetic presence, and clearly knew it.

I would bet anything he knew exactly what to say or do to get people to do what he wanted. Women in particular. Hell, I hadn't exactly tried to resist.

Would I have if I knew who he was? I should have known. He wasn't exactly a regular guy. A person I might meet while walking down the street. He was the lead singer of Wolf Venom. People all over the world knew him on sight.

Me, well, I didn't tend to fangirl over other singers. I listened to them, but most of the time I had no idea what they looked like. I suspected he had no idea who I was either, until Jackson and Penn explained.

What the fuck was Penn's problem anyway? Some people liked being assholes for the heck of it.

If that was his thing, I would have to try to ignore him.

I suspected that might be easier said than done. Especially when we were on tour. It didn't help that he was at least as hot as Zeke. All of the guys were. If I didn't know how good they were as musicians, I might have suspected they were chosen for how attractive they were.

Some might say the same about me, though.

"I'll leave you to it," Jackson said. "Don't worry, you're in good hands."

"Of course she is," Zeke said with one of his panty melting smiles.

God, he made me want to tear off my clothes and jump his bones. Nothing good could come out of him being this hot, I was sure of it. Except a bit of fun.

Was he even up for that now we were working together?

Why was I even thinking this? I should be focusing on the tour and my future. Not to mention my reputation. All of which was based on absolute bullshit. I was used and treated like crap and when they were done with me, they threw me away. If it wasn't for Levi and White Wolf Records...

While I was thinking and staring at Zeke, I hadn't

even realised he'd stepped closer to me, and Jackson left.

"Can you guys give us a minute?" Zeke asked. He waved back towards the corridor.

One of the guys made kissy noises and most of them laughed. No prizes for guessing who scowled instead. Penn looked at me like he wished the ground would open up under my feet and swallow me up.

There was definitely something wrong with me. I found the expression as sexy as hell.

I still sneered back at him and turned away.

We stepped out into the corridor and Zeke closed the door behind us.

"What is this about?" I asked. "Are you going to tell me the guys have talked and you won't work with me?" I leaned my back against the wall and closed my eyes. When was this shit going to start getting easier?

"Not at all." Zeke's voice sounded close to my ear.

When I opened my eyes I saw he pressed his hand to the wall beside my head and leaned in until his breath brushed my cheek. He was so close I could almost feel heat rolling off him in waves. Or maybe that was me.

I looked him right in his eyes. They were vivid

blue, a shade or two darker than mine. I felt as if he could see right into my soul. If he could read my mind he would know I wanted him to touch me so badly it hurt.

I cleared my throat. "I can think of two other things we should probably talk about. I'm not sure the corridor is the right place for either of them."

He sighed and stepped back away from me. "You're right. There's probably a private, empty room around here somewhere."

"That sounds dangerous," I said.

He turned back and grinned. "Oh? It does? I like the sound of that. Maybe we should find somewhere." He stepped back to me and ran the back of his fingers down the side of my cheek and across my lower lip.

He must have felt me trembling.

"Or we could rehearse before they tear up my contract," I said reluctantly. "Was that all you wanted to talk about?"

"In a way." He lowered his voice. "I wanted to say that any time you want to continue what we started the other night, I'm up for it. Mostly, thought, I wanted you to know I got rid of the you-know-what. It's not going to turn back up and cause anyone to point fingers at either of us. We could have been caught on a security camera together so I figured you'd want to know."

"Great." I hadn't even thought of that, but he was right. If the police came after him, they would start looking into me too. That was the last thing I needed. "Thank you."

I cocked my head at him when he looked like he had more to say.

His hand rested lightly on my cheek. "I can't guarantee that won't happen again. Usually, when the other guys are around it doesn't, but sending Jonah after me shows how desperate Reuben is getting. Shit might escalate. I'll do what I can to keep you out of it."

"Have you thought about talking to the police?" I asked.

He looked down at the tiled floor, then back up again. "I can't. That's a conversation for another place. Somewhere we wouldn't be overheard. Let's just say it's not in their best interests to help me or act against Reuben."

"This Reuben guy sounds like a piece of work," I said.

Zeke chuckled. "You could say that, yes." He looked at me like he wanted to kiss me. His lips were only a few centimetres from mine. All I had to do was turn my face…

"Should we go back in?" I asked instead.

"Yeah we should," he said reluctantly. "If we don't, they'll start talking about us." A smile crept onto the corners of his lips. "They'll start to think we're doing naughty things out here."

I laughed softly. "We wouldn't want them to think we're doing *naughty* things."

"They'll get jealous if they think that." He traced circles around the side of my mouth and my chin with the calloused pad of his thumb. "I'm sure they all want to do naughty things with you."

That was interesting. My eyes widened. "All of them?"

"Why not all of them?" His thumb moved down to the side of my throat. If he kept doing that, we were going to *have* to find a private room.

And I'd have to change my panties.

"Because at least one of them hates my guts," I said dryly.

"One day, Penn will get over himself," Zeke assured me. "Believe me when I say his bark is worse than his bite. Although, his bite is pretty shitty."

"I'll say." I wrinkled my nose. "I'm used to guys like him. They're usually threatened by a woman in their space, or have hang ups for whatever reason.

That's their problem, not mine." Although, the tour would be more fun if he checked his bullshit at the door.

"Exactly," he agreed. "Life is too short to deal with other people's shit unless you have to. We're going to have to sit down and talk about what songs you're going to sing with us. Do you want to do that over dinner?"

"Yes," I said a little too fast. "I mean, sure."

He smiled like he was absolutely certain I was going to say yes, no matter what the question.

Part of me wished I said no, just to take him down a peg or two. A guy like him wouldn't stay down for too long though. Besides, it was hard not to like him. He was attractive, charming and at least a little bit dangerous.

I might never admit this, even to myself, but when I got over being scared about the gun in my face, I found it strangely exciting. That was all kinds of wrong, I knew that, but adrenaline had a mind of its own.

"Great." He looked serious. "Are you really staying at that hotel?"

I shrugged. "It was all I could afford."

"I'll speak to Jackson about finding you somewhere better to stay," he said. "Or..." He raised an eyebrow.

"Or?" I prompted.

"You could stay with me," he finished. "I have plenty of room at my place. I even have a spare bedroom if you'd prefer to sleep in there." His brow dropped into a wiggle.

"Is it safe at your place?" I asked, ignoring his not particularly subtle suggestion. "I don't want to wake up in the middle of the night and find a gun in my face."

He leaned in and said, "Sweetheart, if you wake up in the middle of the night and find something in your face, it's not gonna be a gun."

I snorted a laugh. "I should have seen that coming a mile away."

"If you see me coming, I won't be a mile away." His smile widened. "I'll be right there beside you. Or *inside* you."

Between his proximity, the smell of him and the conversation, it was getting more and more difficult to think straight. If we were alone, I would undo his jeans and ride him here and now. I had a feeling he knew that too. Judging by the look he gave me, the feeling was entirely mutual.

"I could use somewhere to stay while I wait for the first paycheck to roll in," I admitted.

I should also hire someone to take care of my finances so I didn't end up in this position again. As soon as I had enough money, I would buy a house and never have to stay in a fleabag hotel again.

"If you're sure you don't mind me sleeping in your spare room." Any other arrangement would feel like I was moving in with the guy. Considering we'd known each other for a matter of hours, that seemed a bit premature.

I was attracted to him, but even I didn't move that fast.

He looked a little disappointed, but nodded. "Of course I don't mind." No doubt he thought the sleeping arrangement was temporary. Maybe it would be.

One thing was for sure, it was going to be difficult to share space with him and keep my hands to myself. I'd never been very good at resisting temptation. Especially in hotter than hell form.

"We should go in and rehearse." He stepped away from me. "After that, I'll help you move your stuff in and we can have a nice dinner out. You look like you could use some spoiling. I fully intend to do just that. If you'll let me."

"I wouldn't say no to being spoiled." He was right, it had been a while. "As long as you don't expect anything in return."

"I never expect anything, especially in return," he said firmly. "But I'm always hopeful." After a moment he added, "And willing."

Yeah, I figured that about him.

6

ABBIE

"Do you know Bump in the Night?" Zeke asked.

"Of course." I nodded. Did anyone *not* know that song? It was all over the radio, top of the streaming apps and featured in fuck knows how many videos on various social media apps. You'd have to live under a rock to not know it.

Zeke nodded to the guys and they started to play.

For a while I forgot about everything and just enjoyed rehearsing with the guys. I didn't know all the lyrics to this particular song, but I knew enough to sing along with the chorus.

"Girl, you're the one I shouldn't touch,
    you're toxic to my soul.

When your hands are all over me,
I just can't fuckin' stop.

YOU MAKE me go bump in the night.
I want to grind you, pound you,
you make me beg for more.
Without your body, I'm nothing."

THE GUYS WEREN'T KNOWN for having subtle songs and wholesome lyrics. Neither was I, to be honest. We would all look pretty strange singing about rainbows and puppies. Unless those puppies were hell hounds and the rainbows were a way of saying we don't care who you fuck, as long as everyone consents.

I was totally here for both of those things.

"That was awesome." Zeke was grinning as a song wound up. "We can give the backing vocalists a song or two off while you sing. Rather than have their voices detract from yours."

"Maybe she could be a backing vocalist," Penn suggested. "Then she could sing on every fucking song."

He was obviously not suggesting it to be nice.

I ignored him.

"Let's take a break," Zeke suggested. He seemed to be the leader of the band as well as the lead singer. Or maybe the other guys were just ready for a break.

Either way, they put down their instruments and Channing handed around bottles of water to everyone.

"Lucky they always provide extras." He handed one to me and his fingers brushed over mine. He looked into my eyes and smiled. And then winked.

He and Landon were the youngest in the band and they were both adorable. Especially when they curled up together on the couch at the back of the room and looked at one of their phones together.

"Cute, aren't they?" Zeke placed a hand on the back of my neck, under my hair. The gesture was casual and possessive at the same time. If it bothered any of the guys, apart from Penn, they didn't give any sign. If anything, they looked curious and none were deterred from looking at my breasts.

"They are," I agreed. "They're…together?" The look Channing gave me confused me as to where they stood.

"More or less," he said. "They're both bi, but they won't sleep with a woman unless they're both involved. Personally, it wouldn't surprise me if they had a three way permanent relationship some day. Or more than three." He shrugged.

That explained the vibe I got from Channing. What would it be like to sleep with both of them? I've done a lot of things with a lot of people but rarely ever a threesome. Certainly never more than that.

"And the others?" I sipped my water and tried not to be too distracted by the way Zeke's fingers traced circles on the back of my neck.

"I believe the term is single and ready to mingle," he said. "You know what this life is like. We're always busy and we spend half the time fending off groupies."

I snorted softly. "Or not fending them off."

"That too," he said unapologetically. "One of the perks to being who we are."

That should absolutely not bother me, but for some reason it did. The thought of him sleeping with someone else sent a flutter of annoyance through me.

I had no right to think like that, or be possessive. Just because he made it clear he wanted to fuck me again, didn't mean he didn't want to fuck the next woman who walked into the room as well.

Same for all of the guys.

I slipped away from him and into one of the comfortable armchairs near the couch.

"How long have you guys been together?"

"About six years," Asher replied. He flopped into the chair to one side of me and Zeke sat in the other. "Zeke and I have known each other most of our lives. We met the other guys at Sydney Uni bar, when we were playing with some other guys."

"What were you called back then?" Tully asked.

Asher winced. "Robot Assholes from Uranus."

I laughed. "I don't know why you didn't keep that name. It's so snappy."

"And almost accurate," Zeke said with a grin. "Fun fact, Landon is an actual robot."

Landon grinned and stuck up his two middle fingers at him. "I'm very sophisticated, and for the record, the term is artificial intelligence."

"I don't know about the intelligence part," Asher teased.

Landon turned his two fingered salute on Asher. "I know you love me."

"Of course I do, dude. No one plays bass like you do." Asher crossed his legs so his ankle rested on his knee.

"You're not going to start being all mushy on each

other are you?" Penn growled. "The way Zeke is staring at that slut is bad enough."

"This from the guy who fucks anything if it's still for long enough," Tully said. "Including the receptionist in the break room on the way in this morning."

"That explains why she wasn't at the desk when I arrived," Zeke said.

In the interest of not responding angrily to Penn's insult, I pulled out my phone and started doing a little digging.

When I realised all of the guys' eyes were on me, I started to read out loud. "Beauregard Pennington. That's a mouthful. Sydney Boys Grammar. Ohhh, fancy." Apparently his parents had some money.

"What are you doing?" Penn growled.

Without looking up, I said, "You looked me up. It's only fair that I return the favour." I went on reading. "Full scholarship to Sydney Conservatory of Music. Dropped out after a year. Isn't that a shame?" My eyes widened at the next sentence. "Found—"

"Abbie," Zeke said, his tone a clear warning.

I looked up at him and he shook his head.

"Don't. It's…in the past." His gorgeous blue eyes flicked towards Penn in worry, then back to me.

I turned off my phone. If Penn asked me to shut up, I wouldn't have, but for Zeke I did.

If nothing else, I owed him for saving me from getting shot in the head. Besides, what I read was pretty horrible and nothing anyone needed to relive. Not even Penn.

"Thank you," Zeke said softly. In a louder voice he said, "As you can tell, when young Penn met us, he was on a path to greatness. We dragged him there via a dirtier route. Otherwise, he would be stuck playing classical piano in front of audiences with their noses in the air."

"Fuck that," Penn muttered.

There was obviously a lot more to this story, but I sensed I wasn't going to get it today.

"So you all grew up in Sydney?" I asked.

"Zeke and I did," Asher said. "And Penn and Tully. Landon is originally from Brisbane. Channing is a Melbourne boy."

"Me too," I said. "I mean, from Melbourne. I'm not a boy." Trust me to say something so silly. I was trying to make a good impression on them and I wasn't sure it was working. One hated me and now the rest probably thought I was an idiot.

"You're definitely not a boy," Zeke agreed. The look he gave me made me want to straddle his lap and ride his cock, even though there were five other guys in the room.

They could watch if they wanted to. That idea was hotter than hell.

"What am I sensing here?" Asher asked. "Do you two know each other? There's been a vibe between you since Abbie walked into Jackson's office. At first I thought it was just Zeke being hot for Abbie, like he's hot for anyone with nipples. But the more I look at you both, the more I think something is up." He narrowed his eyes and cocked his head at us.

I didn't know how to answer that. Fortunately, Zeke saved me from having to.

"Sometimes two people connect," he said lightly. "Abbie seems lovely and, personally, I'd like to get to know her a lot better. Wouldn't all of you like the same thing?"

"Of course we would," Asher said. "And we will. We're all going to be working *very* closely together for the next few months. The best thing we can do is all get along to the satisfaction of everyone."

My eyes swivelled to him and he smiled. Yeah, I noticed the innuendos in his words. And the way his hazel eyes lingered on mine.

Where Zeke was dark, Asher was blond, with

light hair and skin. Even with a tan, he was paler than Zeke. He was at least as ripped as Zeke.

What would it be like to be in the middle of the two of them? Their hands all over me. Their cocks in my pussy and mouth.

Shit, if I kept thinking like this it was going to be difficult to get *any* work done.

I reminded myself what was at stake here. The label gave me a chance to resurrect my career. I wasn't going to get a third chance. I had to make this work or I was screwed.

"Working closely together," Penn muttered. "I can't hardly fucking wait."

I was tempted to turn my phone back on and keep reading, or throw the device at his head. For Zeke's sake, and my phone's, I did neither of those things. I couldn't afford to replace my phone if I broke it anyway.

"Of course you can't," I said instead. "Sooner or later you're going to realise how awesome I am." I didn't think I was all that awesome, but there was something about him that made me want to provoke him.

He barked a laugh. "I hope this tour does mother-fucking wonders for your career. Then you can piss off and leave us alone."

For a moment, I thought he was going to be nice. I should have known better. My bad.

"I'm curious about something," I said slowly. "Did you drop out of the Conservatory of Music, or were you kicked out for being an asshole?"

What? It was a legitimate question. They shouldn't have to put up with his bullshit any more than I did.

"I left because concert pianists don't have horny groupies with hungry pussies." Penn smirked. "Not as many as rock gods do anyway."

I shrugged. "That's as good a reason for dropping out as any." I wondered if Tully's suggestion that Penn would sleep with anyone who crossed his path was accurate. I suspected it was, making his suggestion that I was a slut more than a little bit hypocritical.

Whatever, I didn't care what he did with his sex life. I certainly wasn't going to apologise for enjoying sex. Especially not to him.

"I thought so," Penn said.

That was the first almost civil thing he said to me since we met. There might be hope for him after all.

"Not that I need your fucking approval," he added.

Or maybe there wasn't.

"Are we going to finish rehearsal?" Tully asked. "As *stimulating* as this conversation is..." He gave me a wink.

Yeah, I didn't miss that innuendo either. Working with Wolf Venom was either going to be a lot of fun, or a bunch of really, really long months.

7

ZEKE

MOVING Abbie into my spare room didn't take long. The whole undertaking consisted of rolling two small suitcases from her hotel to my inner-city townhouse. Piece of cake, even though she winced when paying the hotel bill. I would have offered to settle it for her, but I suspected she'd refuse.

"Home, sweet home." I unlocked the door and did a quick visual sweep inside before I let her in. I saw no sign of Jonah, or any other immediate threats. They'd have to get past my security system anyway.

Good luck with that, I thought. It was the latest, best money could buy.

I rolled her case over the threshold and closed the door behind her.

"Nice place." She glanced around.

"Thanks. It's nothing fancy." It was typical for the area. Expensive, with a view of nothing in particular, but it was convenient to all the pubs, clubs and restaurants.

I bought it a couple of years ago and had it totally remodelled. Tastefully, of course. I'd leave purple walls and gold fixtures and fittings to the other guys.

I preferred light hardwood floors and neutral paint on the walls.

Nothing I couldn't look at if I was hung over.

I took the other suitcase from her and carried both up the stairs. They felt like she stashed a few bricks in there. Maybe she did. Who knew with women?

"I've thought about getting away from the city to have more space, but this place is convenient and it doesn't take my housekeeper long to clean." I grinned over my shoulder. "What the hell would I do with six or seven bedrooms anyway?"

"Is that a rhetorical question?" she asked with a laugh.

I reached the top of the stairs. "It wasn't supposed to be, but I see you've interpreted it in a different way from how I intended. At least, I think you did." I quirked an eyebrow in question. "You are implying I should put six or seven women in those bedrooms, weren't you?"

She laughed. "Them, or your bandmates."

Interesting that was where her mind went. Was that the kind of relationship she was after?

"We would need two or three housekeepers then." I put her suitcases down to the side of my spare room and shook out my arms. "It's not the biggest room in the world."

It looked smaller, still furnished with a timber framed double bed, two matching bedside tables and a small wardrobe.

"It's a lot nicer than the hotel," she said.

Yeah, she was right there. Charging people to stay in places like that should be illegal. My place wasn't huge, but it was neat and clean. Five stars compared to that dump.

"There's a bathroom on the other side of the corridor." I nodded towards it. "You have it all to yourself. Unless you don't want to."

I wanted to slip a hand under her hair, to the back of her neck, and kiss her. She smelled like an intoxicating combination of rose soap and some kind of floral shampoo. Good enough to eat. I was aching to taste her mouth. I bet she tasted divine.

Instead, I said, "There should be hangers in the

wardrobe. Make yourself comfortable. There's no hurry for you to move out. You can stay until you're ready."

It wasn't until I saw her suitcases that I realised how tough things were for her right now. I suspected everything she owned in the world was inside them.

If that was the case, she *really* needed the opportunity the label gave her. I would do everything in my power to make sure it worked out the way she needed it to. Whatever it took.

I thought I saw a tear on her cheek, but she wiped away before I could be sure.

"Thank you. You've been really sweet. Sweeter than I deserve."

That was definitely a tear she wiped away the second time.

"Hey." I put my hands on her shoulders and turned her gently to face me.

"You deserve to have people be nice to you and take care of you. You're beautiful, smart and talented. Onyx Riot didn't do right by you, but White Wolf Records will. I promise. And Wolf Venom will look after you. You're one of us now."

Honestly, I wanted to find the owner of her former label and punch him in the face. And whoever the asshole was that faked a marriage to her.

Who even does shit like that?

Judging by Penn's snide comments, it wouldn't take more than a minute or two of searching on the Internet to find the answer.

I made a mental note to do that later. Not because I wanted to intrude on her privacy, but because I knew people who could beat the crap out of other people if I asked them to.

All right, I knew people that could do a lot worse than that, but a warning should be enough.

Unless they hurt her again. Then all bets were off. There wasn't anything I wouldn't do to protect the people I cared about, including the rest of the band.

Yes, even Penn. He wasn't so bad when you got to know him.

"Okay?" I said softly. "You deserve to be safe and happy."

She sniffed and nodded. "Thank you. You and the label have been so incredible. You couldn't be any different to Onyx Riot. I know they have a business to run, but they treated me like I was a commodity." She shook her head. "White Wolf feels more like a family."

I gave her a lopsided smile. "Sometimes we're dysfunctional, but I like to think of us as family. When we're on tour, we hang out with the support act and all the tour staff. No one is above or below anyone else. Unless they're fucking."

She let out a choked little laugh before her expression turned serious. "Is that the catch here? You be nice to me in return for me fucking you?"

Ouch. The suggestion stung my ego a tiny bit. Did I really seem like the kind of guy who put conditions on being nice? Or was it that she was screwed so badly over in the past it was easier to make that assumption than think anyone actually gave a shit?

I didn't want to admit it, but it made sense. She was living in my house, albeit temporarily. Some guys wouldn't do that without expecting something in return.

"There's no catch," I said firmly. "I in no way expect you to sleep with me. You needed a place to stay, I was happy to offer. That's all. Anything that happens between us, if it does, is entirely up to you. This is a no strings attached situation."

I had some rope and a pair of handcuffs if she wanted to be tied up, but those were unrelated to her staying here with me.

She looked sceptical, but nodded. "Okay. I appreciate that."

I bent to kiss her cheek and stepped back. "I'll leave you to get settled in. I'll book us in for somewhere to have dinner tonight. Is there anything you prefer to eat?"

She lowered her eyes and looked right at my groin. A slow smile crept onto her face.

"I also like most foods. The hotter, the better." Was she talking about food, my cock or both?

"I like it hot too." And now my jeans were tight at the front. I wanted to grab her, tear off her clothes and push her down on the bed. I wanted to bury myself balls deep inside her. I wanted to come in her so hard she overflowed. I wanted to taste every centimetre of her and feel her mouth all over me.

I wanted…

Fuck, after my reassurance that she wasn't obliged to sleep with me, I couldn't make the first move, not right now. No matter how badly I wanted to.

Even though my balls hurt like hell. I *had* to wait until the right time.

She raised her eyes. There was something in the depths, like she desperately wanted to believe me.

I felt like this was some kind of test. One I didn't

want to fail. If I did, I may never regain her trust. I wanted—needed—her to know I was sincere.

"I should unpack." She eyed the suitcases sadly. "It shouldn't take long."

"Right." I nodded. "Take your time. I'll put on the coffee machine for some real coffee."

"I like the sound of that," she said. Her eyes were brighter now, eager. Coffee had that effect on people. "I haven't had a real coffee in ages."

I grinned. "Then you're in for a treat. I have very particular taste in beans and the best way to brew them." Which was my way of saying I was a coffee snob. I only drank the instant stuff the label provided because that was all there was.

One of these days, I was going to take my own in. On the other hand, then I would have to share it. Maybe instant wasn't so bad.

I gave her a lingering look. Even in the face of impending coffee, it was hard to tear myself away from her. She was like a gorgeous magnet, drawing me to her.

If I wasn't careful, I would find myself falling for her.

That was dangerous in so many ways. Because we worked together. Because I had a reputation for sticking my cock in every hole I could find.

A reputation that wasn't undeserved.

I liked sex. As a single guy, I had few reasons to refuse when it was offered and it was offered often. For some reason, women seemed to like fucking rock stars.

I certainly wasn't complaining. All those women kept life interesting and my cock happy.

Mostly though, falling for her would be dangerous thanks to Reuben and my past.

If that caught up to me, worse things could happen to her than a gun shoved in her face. Reuben wouldn't hesitate to use her to get to me. Reuben wouldn't hesitate to use anyone I knew to get to me. The fact he hadn't, meant he wasn't completely desperate. Not yet.

It was coming, as inevitably as the sunset. I needed to find a way to stay out of his path. Permanently.

Whatever happened, I wasn't going back. That was a dark part of my life I wanted to put behind me and forget.

"Wait," Abbie said before I stepped out of the room.

When I turned, she put a hand on my arm and stood on her toes to lightly brush her lips over mine.

When she moved away and crouched beside her suitcases, I asked, "What was that for?"

And why in hell was it hotter than a deep, passionate kiss or a blow job?

"I just wanted to," she said lightly. "That's all."

I smiled and nodded. "Well, thank you. I'll be downstairs if you need me." I hurried away before I changed my mind about leaving her by herself.

Think about coffee, I told myself. *Maybe really cold coffee.*

Fuck, having her here was going to be...interesting, to say the least.

8

ZEKE

"OH MY GOD, you weren't wrong about the coffee." She closed her eyes and looked blissed out.

"Of course. I'm never wrong about coffee." I watched her face and admired the height of her cheekbones, the curve of her chin, the way her nose turned up at the end. The sprinkling of freckles around her nose might be the cutest thing I ever saw.

"I know a thing or two about wine, beer and tequila," I added. For example, I knew tequila tasted better when licked off a woman's skin than it did drunk from a glass.

Although, what didn't taste better licked off skin?

She opened her eyes and we both spoke at the same time.

"So about Reuben..."

"So about the twenty-six hour marriage..."

We both smiled, but I had to concede the point to her.

"I owe you an explanation." I sat back on the couch and rested my ankle on my opposite knee.

"You don't necessarily owe me anything," she said slowly. "I would like to know why someone was holding a gun to my head."

"Yeah, that's fair." I cleared my throat. "Reuben is my brother. He's the oldest of seven. All boys. Reuben, Caleb and Joshua are from my father's first wife. She died under circumstances which are still not clear."

According to the police that was. I didn't have much doubt about what really happened.

"My parents got married three months after she died and I was born three months later."

"So either you were premature or..." Abbie's eyes widened.

"Or my mother was already pregnant when my father's first wife died," I finished for her. "Hint, I wasn't premature."

"Oh my god," she whispered. "You think your father got her out of the way?"

"He did, or he had someone to do it for him." I

grimaced. "Or maybe it was a convenient accident. Either way, my father was known for having multiple mistresses, so he wouldn't have been alone for long no matter what went down."

I took a sip of coffee. "So then I was born, then Lucas and finally the twins, Hunter and Parker."

"That's a lot of boys," she said.

"Yep, and we range from thirty-nine down to nineteen." I sat a bit below the middle of that range.

"So that's why Reuben thinks he's your father," she said. "Because he's so much older."

"That and he inherited my father's place as head of the family when he died. A fact he likes to remind us of as often as he can." I rolled my eyes.

"And by family you don't just mean a group of related people, do you?" she asked tentatively.

"No," I agreed. "Whatever assumption you want to make about what they're into, you're probably right. I won't go into detail because if, for whatever reason, the police ask questions, it's better you have no answers to give them. For your safety."

I didn't want her getting into trouble because of me or my family, and it was hard to know who might be on the payroll. My brother's reach was wide.

"Okay, but can you tell me who Jonah is?" she asked. "Is he a relative?"

"Fuck no. Jonah is just hired muscle. He does odd jobs for my brother, like threatening people."

"And killing people?" she whispered as though she was scared there was someone outside the window, listening.

"Probably." I nodded slowly.

"So if your brother told him to kill us, he would have done that?" She looked more pissed off than scared.

I could understand that. If she died just because she was in my company, I would be irritated too.

"He would have killed me," I agreed. "He would have killed you if Reuben told him to make sure there weren't any witnesses."

"So when he threatened to kill me—" She frowned.

"He would have been going off script," I said. "He would have had instructions not to kill me, but they wouldn't have extended to you. No offence, but Reuben never cared much about collateral damage."

"That might be the worst *no offence but* I've ever heard," she said dryly. "No offence, but my brother doesn't give a shit if you get murdered."

"I'm sorry if I gave you the impression my brother was anything other than an asshole," I said sarcastically. "He's a ruthless bastard who will step on anyone and everyone to get his way. Including his brothers."

"Why does he want you back so badly?" she asked.

I grunted. "Because he hates the fact I'm out here living my life. He wants me to be the dutiful brother, doing whatever he tells me to do. I'm not interested in being his hired muscle."

She looked at me for a long moment and then burst out laughing.

I frowned at her. "What?"

It took her a minute or two to compose herself so she could respond.

"I'm sorry, I was imagining what it would be like if you tried to approach someone like Jonah did. Don't get me wrong, you'd be terrifying with a gun in your hand." She shivered lightly. "But then if they recognised you, they would probably ask for an autograph or a selfie. And then later when they realised what was really going on, they would know exactly how to describe you to the police."

I flicked a finger gun in her direction. "Excellent point. I'll have to remember to tell Reuben that the next time I talk to him. I'm way too recognisable to get away with anything."

"Would he leave you alone if he realised that?" she asked.

"That wouldn't work for a minute," I admitted. "He'd probably tell me to wear a mask or grow a beard." I preferred designer scruff that made me look just messy enough, without the hassle of having to trim a beard.

"Or he'd give me a job behind the scenes. Knowing him, he'd get off on having me drive him around everywhere or some shit like that. Or collecting money from one of his brothels."

Being an asshole, he wouldn't let me touch any of the staff, even if I paid. Not that I would ever pay for sex. I hadn't needed to yet, I didn't intend to start doing it.

"That doesn't sound as glamorous as being a rock star." She said the last word and her breath fell into a sigh. "Although, that can be overrated."

She looked so sad I wanted to kiss her heartache away.

"Which brings me to my question," I said tentatively. "You don't have to talk about it if you don't want to." I hadn't looked her up. I decided against it. Whatever she wanted me to know, she could tell me and I would listen. The rest was none of my business.

Until my curiosity got the better of me.

"There's not much to say." She shrugged. "Boy meets girl. Girl falls in love with boy. Boy suggests they elope. Girl agrees. Boy admits the marriage was just to further his career. Girl gets annulment. Boy doesn't get a broken nose, although he deserved it."

She let out a longer, heavier sigh.

"It wasn't Penn, was it?" I couldn't resist asking.

She looked surprised, but then burst out laughing. "God no. Although now you mention it, there was a resemblance between them. They were both ambitious assholes."

"I'm sorry someone thought it was okay to do that to you." I thought about sneaking in a good word for Penn, because the guy had his moments, but he could stick up for himself.

And no doubt he would the next time we were all together.

"I just wish the publicity helped my career," she said. "Instead, it made me look like an idiot. And then there was the whole affair thing." She used air quotes. "Sometimes I think I shouldn't be let out unsupervised. Apparently I make really crappy choices when I'm left to my own devices."

I scooted over closer to her. "I don't know, I've only seen you make good choices so far."

I hesitated and hoped she wasn't about to stab me in the ego, when I asked, "You don't regret what we did in the club, do you?"

"Not for a minute," she said firmly. "That was... memorable. You could have been a jerk about it, but you weren't. At least, not that I've seen." She gave me a speculative look.

"If by that you mean tell the guys or spill everything to a tabloid, no. I haven't done either of those. What happened between us is just between us. Unless we agree otherwise."

"I'd prefer if the tabloids don't know." She wrinkled her nose. "I've given them more than enough ammunition over the years. The guys, well, it doesn't worry me if they know. I have nothing to be ashamed of. And honestly, it might be easier if there aren't any secrets between you and them."

That took me by surprise. Most women seemed hellbent on keeping their sex lives secret. I guessed when yours was as open as hers was in the past, there was no point in trying to pretend it didn't exist.

She frowned and changed the subject. "Do the other guys know about your family?"

"Yeah," I replied. "Especially Asher. Like I said, he and I have known each other all our lives. His family and mine are intertwined somewhat. Although, right now his is..." I searched for the right words. "In disgrace, in a manner of speaking. His father pissed off the wrong people, so all of the DiMarco family are on the outs as far as the Brantley and Bell families are concerned."

"Bell family?" she echoed. "How many families are there?"

I shrugged one shoulder. "In this country? A few, but the most powerful are the Brantleys and the Bells. And to a lesser extent, the Fiorellis. They're all bitter rivals. For the record, if you think Reuben is bad, he has nothing on the Bells. They are as ruthless and depraved as they come. Most of them would traffic their own mothers for money."

"How charming," she said sarcastically. "I'm starting to think the people at Onyx Riot were actually nice."

I smiled. "It's all relative, I guess. No pun intended."

"Are you sure?" she asked.

I knitted my brows. "Am I sure of what?"

"Are you sure you didn't intend that pun? It

sounded intentional to me." The side of her mouth quirked upwards.

I laughed. "Okay, you caught me. It was a little bit intentional. If I don't laugh about my family, I might cry. Sometimes I wish I was born into a normal family, like Channing's, or even Penn's. Asher and I got the short straw there."

"I had a normal family," she said softly. "And my life still ended up fucked up. At least you have your head on straight."

"One of my heads is straight. The other slants a little to the left." I grinned.

"I remember," she said with a nod. "And it's very tasty too."

In spite of my resolve to wait, I couldn't help myself.

"You know what else is tasty?" I took a sip of coffee and leaned towards her. I slanted my mouth over hers and carefully pried her lips open with my tongue.

When she opened her mouth, I slowly squirted the coffee inside. Then kissed her lightly for good measure.

I leaned away and hoped she wasn't about to hurt me. Not that a little thing like her could do me much damage, unless she dug her knee into my groin.

To my intense relief, she smiled and swallowed.

"That *was* tasty." She licked her lips. "There might not be anything hotter than a guy who shares his coffee, especially like that."

"I can think of something hotter than that," I said. "You."

She blushed adorably.

It was too late for me to be careful. I was already falling for her.

9

ABBIE

"CAN YOU SPEAK ITALIAN?" I was a bit uneasy on my feet after several glasses of wine.

At some point during the walk home, Zeke's hand slipped into mine. I didn't pull away.

"No," he said with a laugh. "That's another reason why I'd make a terrible mobster. Can't speak Italian."

He was at least as tipsy as I was. "Asher on the other hand. He's fluent. Or is it French?" He snapped his fingers. "Actually, I think it's both. What a show off, ay?"

I laughed softly. "If you've got it, flaunt it."

"That's always been my motto." He swung our hands between us before pulling me closer to his side.

"You've certainly got it." He let my hand go and

snaked an arm around my waist. He pulled me closer still and nuzzled his face into the side of my neck.

"You smell so good." He drew me to a stop and lightly ran the tip of his tongue from just under my ear, to my throat. "Taste good too."

I couldn't hold back the moan that slipped from between my lips.

He manoeuvred me a couple of steps until my back was pressed against a slender tree. Then his hands were up the back of my shirt and my hands were up the front of his.

He kissed his way up my throat, over my chin to my mouth. When our lips met, it was like an explosion of fireworks. His stubble tickled pleasantly.

He slid his hands around to ghost over my stomach and up to cup my breasts. He palmed my nipples through the thin fabric of my bra. They rose to tight, hard peaks in response.

Blood pounded through me like thunder. I wanted to feel every part of him on and in me. Not just because he turned me on, but because I was drawn to him. Zeke the person, not Zeke Brantley the rock star. He was sweet and sexy, even with that edge of danger around him and his family.

If I had any sense, I would stay away after what he told me about his brother, but I didn't want to stay away. Not from him and not from any of the other guys either.

I wanted to get to know all of them at some point. Yeah, even Penn. I was almost certain there was a decent guy under his exterior, albeit deep down.

Zeke drew his hand out, and peeled down the front of my shirt and the cup of my bra. He leaned in to run his tongue in circles around and over my nipple.

I was already panting out my nose before he did that. My panties were ruined.

The more I was around him, the more I realised this was going to be a permanent thing.

He only had to touch me to make me hot, much less touch me like this. And we barely even started.

He suckled for a while, before peeling back the left cup and sucking on that nipple.

I reached a hand down between us and over the front of his pants. Instead of his usual jeans, he'd worn dress pants and a dark blue button down shirt. His cock was now straining to get out of the front of those pants.

I was happy to oblige.

I undid the button, slid down the zipper and slipped my hand inside. Why was I not even slightly surprised to learn he went commando tonight? Not surprised, but pleased.

I curled my fingers around his already rock hard length.

He groaned. "Sweetheart, the way you make me feel..." He looked up at me and grinned. "I want to do so many naughty things to you."

I smiled back. "I want you to do all the naughty things to me."

His eyebrows rose slightly. "*All* the naughty things? I can think of lots and lots of them. That's just off the top of my head."

"Which head?" I circled the tip of his cock with my finger.

His breath hitched. "Both of them. But you're making it hard for the head on my shoulders to think."

He worked his hands under my skirt and grabbed my ass. My G-string left my cheeks bare to his warm, calloused skin.

"That's the idea," I said, my voice husky. "Thinking is overrated." Says the woman who got in a lot of trouble from not thinking in the past.

That felt like a different lifetime and a different person. Zeke was not my ex-lover or my ex-husband, if I could even call either of them that. He was a better person than both of them combined. Hell, Penn was a better person than both of them.

That yardstick was very fucking low.

"It really is," Zeke agreed. He glanced around me. "I don't think that tree is up to me fucking you against it. I intend to pound you harder than that."

That sent a shiver through me, so hot I was almost ready to come on the spot. He was right though. It was already bending with me pressed lightly against it.

"I would prefer no flora or fauna were harmed in the making of this session," I said. "Not to mention it might piss your neighbours off."

"That's true." He cupped my cheeks a little tighter and lifted me until my legs wrapped around his waist.

I let out a little squeak of surprise and flung my arms around his neck as well.

He chuckled and carried me up the street toward his place. Or was it our place for now?

Either way, he carried me through the front gate and froze.

"Shit."

I clung on tighter when I thought he was about to drop me. "What is it?"

He stepped back out the gate and lowered me to

the ground. "I don't know. Stay here." He tucked his cock back into his pants and did them up.

I pulled my bra and the front of my dress back into place and watched him step back through the gate. Of course, I followed him. Whatever was going on here, I wasn't going to stand back and wait for it to happen. If he thought it was safe enough to get closer, then surely it was safe enough for me?

He crouched down beside something which lay on the ground near the front door.

"What is that?" I asked while looking over his shoulder.

He startled and looked back at me. "I could have sworn I said to stay back."

I shrugged unapologetically. "Yeah, well, I'm here now. What is it?"

It looked like nothing more terrifying than a cardboard box. I mean, some people might find them scary but I didn't. Until I added, "Is it ticking?"

He leaned in and listened. "No. Not that I can hear."

"Is there any chance someone sent you a cake?" I asked. If they had, I was going to spread some on myself and ask him to lick it all off. And of course I was going to put a bunch of it on him as well. How else would a person eat cake?

"It wouldn't be the weirdest thing I've ever had delivered to me." He sniffed. "It doesn't smell like cake." In the glow from the nearby streetlight, he looked a little sick.

"You should probably not see this," he said.

I hesitated. "I have a feeling you might be right, but I am in it this far. If it's not going to explode, then how bad can it be?"

"Bad," he said. Grimacing, he peeled back the lid.

As soon as he did that, the smell hit my nose.

"Oh my God. Is that…hair?" My stomach twisted into a knot. It wasn't just hair, it was hair attached to a head.

"Who is that?" Did I even want to know?

Zeke reached in gingerly and turned the head until the face was visible. "Jesus Christ," he whispered.

"Is that Jonah?" I asked.

"It was," Zeke agreed. He turned the hired muscle's face away so we couldn't see it. "Not so much anymore."

"Yeah. I don't know, but it doesn't look like he's been dead for long." I'd never seen a dead person before, so what the hell did I know?

"Long enough to be cold, but not too long," Zeke agreed. He closed the lid of the box.

"Is this another message from Reuben?" The expression on Zeke's face had me worried.

He glanced up at me. "No. Reuben doesn't tend to kill his own men. At least, not like this. And he wouldn't leave it here for me to see."

"He might have left for someone else to see?" I looked back over my shoulder, but I didn't see an army of police cars converging on the area. If anyone wanted to set Zeke up, this would be one way to do it. Albeit an extreme one.

Zeke shook his head. "This isn't Reuben's style at all."

"Okay, if it isn't his, then whose is it?" Did I really want the answer to that? How many dangerous people did this guy know?

"I have absolutely no idea," he admitted. "Whoever it is, Reuben is going to be pissed. I need to deal with this and I'm going to have to talk to him before he assumes I'm behind Jonah's disappearance."

His tone sent shivers through me.

"Deal with that?" I asked. "How the fuck are you going to deal with a disembodied head?"

He pulled out his phone and tapped the screen before he shoved it back in his pocket. He picked up the box and stood. "I know a guy."

"Of course you do." I ran a hand over my hair.

"First a gun and now a head. What's next? Is this just another day in the life of Zeke Brantley?"

"No. Usually it's much more interesting than this," he said sarcastically.

I snorted. I was starting to wonder if me being associated with Wolf Venom was some kind of joke. A sick joke at that. My former label might be having a good laugh at my expense. If it wasn't for the smell coming from the box, I might assume the head was fake and all of this was a practical joke. It certainly *smelled* real. I was sober now, but my dinner staying in my stomach was a fifty-fifty shot right now.

"I should get this dealt with." He nodded toward the box. "My friend is only a couple of blocks away."

"I'm coming with you," I said without thinking.

"It's late—" he started.

"I don't care," I said firmly. "I need to know it's really dealt with." And on some level, I needed to know if all of this was actually real. I glanced around for cameras, but didn't see any. Of course, I wouldn't if they were hidden.

A significant part of me wished this *was* a joke. That Zeke wasn't carrying a real head in a cardboard box in his arms. I'd handled humiliation before, I could do it again.

Unfortunately, I was almost certain this was real.

I thought about asking to take a closer look at the head, to be sure, but for once, a bit of common sense kicked in. I already couldn't unsee what I'd seen. A better view would only make those memories stick in my head for longer.

"Besides," I added, "I don't want to be here alone if someone is walking around cutting off heads and sticking them in boxes. Not to mention there might be other parts of Jonah lying around." For all I knew, the rest of him was sitting inside the townhouse on the couch. I didn't want to be alone if I saw that. I mean, I didn't want to see that at all, but certainly not by myself.

Zeke sighed. "Okay then. Let's get this over with."

10

ABBIE

THE LAST PERSON I expected to see when we walked through the front gate of another terraced house was Asher. His expression was as grim as Zeke's.

He peeled open the box's lid and peered inside. "Ahhh, yeah. He's dead all right."

Zeke snorted. "You think? I know some people can function pretty well without having much in the way of brains, but this dude is missing a bit more than that."

Asher closed the lid and shrugged. "You didn't give me specifics in your text message. I was half expecting to turn up with an unconscious person over your shoulder."

"Is that something he does normally?" I asked.

Asher grinned. "It's Zeke, who can tell? He does some pretty wild things."

I should absolutely not find that adorable right now, but I did. I never claimed to be appropriate. I was almost certain there wasn't a right or wrong way to behave in a situation like this anyway. Some people vomit.

Others…get turned on apparently.

"So I've heard," I said dryly. I was hoping he'd assure me this was out of the ordinary.

"This gives a whole new meaning to giving head," Asher said. "Any idea who it's from?"

"Nope. Probably not Reuben but I don't know where to start on making a list of who it might actually be. The only ones who know about this are the three of us, the rest of the band and Reuben."

"Is it possible he has a traitor working for him, or something?" I asked. "Is that even a thing?"

"It's a thing," Asher agreed. "Ask my father. Actually you can't, he double crossed Zeke's father, so he's not alive to tell the story."

Was I hearing right? Zeke's father murdered Asher's father?

What in the world had I gotten myself into? I wasn't sure, but I had a feeling getting out of it was going to be harder than getting in. It would be a lot easier if these guys weren't so fucking attractive.

Yep, there I went, thinking with my clit again.

"If whoever did this is working for Reuben, they're going to end up dead," Zeke said. "Which ultimately is not my problem. My problem is the fact I'm holding a body part in a cardboard box."

"That certainly is a problem," Asher agreed. "I think Haru is in. If anyone can deal with that he can." He turned and rapped on the door with his knuckles before pushing it open.

I sighed softly to myself and followed them inside. This was not how I thought my night would end. I was hoping for more sweat, more panting and a lot more of Zeke's cock inside my pussy.

Not dealing with a severed head with a couple of guys who knew more about mobsters than it was probably healthy to know. When I first met them, I thought they were your average, arrogant rock stars. That wasn't even the start of it. Not even the tip of the proverbial iceberg.

Fucking fuck.

The townhouse was small and narrow, like Zeke's. Unlike his, it was lit entirely with candles. Either this Haru guy loved candlelight, or didn't like electricity. Maybe he didn't have electricity.

That theory was thrown out when we stepped into a back room. Several fridges hummed with energy and an electric coffee maker bubbled away. The scent of the delicious brew filled the air.

A guy of around my height—relatively short—with black hair and dark eyes looked up as we entered the room.

His body was slender to the point of being skinny. He wore black jeans and a bright purple T-shirt with the Rock Dragons logo on the front. If I remembered right, they were an American rock band, almost as popular as Wolf Venom.

"Twice in one week," he commented. His accent sounded faintly Japanese. "I'm going to start to think you're crushing on me."

Zeke chuckled. "I would totally crush on you if you were my type."

"Liar," Haru said playfully. He held out his hands and Zeke handed him the box. "Did you bring me a cake? I'm allergic to chocolate."

"Not a cake," Zeke said ruefully.

Haru opened the box and peered inside. "Definitely not a cake." He put the box over on a table. "Where's the rest of him?"

Zeke shrugged. "No idea. Could be at the bottom

of the harbour for all I know. I'm hoping we don't get any more presents like this."

"Why?" Asher grinned. "Who doesn't want to get a bit of head once in a while? I know I do."

"Great," Zeke said ironically. "The next time someone drops a disembodied head off on my doorstep, I will give it to you."

"Thanks, but I'll pass," Asher said predictably. "I'll take the other kind any day though." He gave me a speculative look.

All I could do right now was smile back, although my eyes did drop to his groin.

He was obviously getting the same vibe I was. I was as attracted to him as I was to Zeke. If it was him in that club the other night, I would have been just as happy to have my lips around his cock. I had a feeling I would get the opportunity before too much longer, if he had his way.

I managed to tear my eyes away from the tent in his jeans and looked over to Haru.

"How are you going to get rid of that?" Clearly my morbid curiosity got the better of me.

"I have a few methods," he said as though he was talking about how to cook a chicken. "Acid. Hammer. Walk to the harbour and throw it in. One time, I got a ride in a helicopter and threw some evidence out the door. We were right over the middle of the Pacific Ocean. That was fucking *cool*." He dragged out the last word.

Asher and Zeke both looked like they were trying to hold back laughter.

I had no idea if Haru was being serious or not. He sounded like he was living his best life either way.

"In this case, something more subtle. We can't have this guy's head bobbing up and coming back to haunt us." He turned away and grabbed a pair of gloves.

"I hadn't thought about being haunted, but now I have. I'm scared." I didn't really believe in ghosts, but if anyone was going to have a vengeful spirit, it was going to be a guy whose remains were disposed of like he was little more than rubbish.

I almost felt sorry for the guy. Almost. A proper funeral was probably never on the cards for him anyway, with his lifestyle, but now he had no choice to redeem himself. Would he have anyway? I had no answers to that.

Zeke and Asher laughed even harder.

I looked over at them. "What?"

Zeke shook his head. "I'm sorry. It's just this whole situation. And how cute you are when you talk about ghosts." He turned to Asher. "She's cute, isn't she?"

Asher gave me a lingering, hungry look. "She certainly is." He glanced at Zeke with the same look in his eyes.

I thought he was going to say something else, but the moment was interrupted by Haru picking up the box and depositing it, cardboard, head and all into a giant oven. The kind they use for cremations. That made sense. Jonah certainly couldn't bob back up when he was just ashes.

Haru swung the oven door closed and locked it.

I felt a twinge of guilt. Sure this Jonah guy threatened to kill me, but he was dead and his family might never know what happened. Was that fair to them, or were they in this as deeply as he was?

Either way, didn't they deserve to know?

I realised there was absolutely nothing I could do about it. At this point, I was in this as much as Asher and Zeke were. If the police found out about it, I would be just as fucked as them. Like it or not, I was going to have to keep my mouth very shut.

"Are you going to tell the rest of the guys about this?" I asked softly.

Zeke nodded with no hesitation. "What you said about not keeping secrets extends to things like this. We can't rule out the possibility this isn't just aimed at me. Someone might have seen us with Jonah and decided to make some point about the band."

I felt my face pale. "It might be about me." I hadn't even thought about that but the possibility was terrifying.

It was Asher who put his arm around me. "If it is, we won't let anything bad happen to you. It's a good thing you're staying with Zeke right now. He's good at kicking asses. Almost as good as me, and I only live a street away."

That explained why he got there so quickly when Zeke texted him.

"That house with six or seven bedrooms is sounding better," Zeke said. "If we were all there, we could all keep Abbie safe. In the meantime, I'll keep an eye on her." He gave me a look like he planned to keep a whole lot of other things on me.

That was fine by me. Finding Jonah's head was like a bucket of cold water poured on us, but it hadn't completely put out the embers. Not to mention, it would be nice to have something to take my mind off all of this for a while.

I was curious about how Haru got rid of the gun, but I decided against asking. I already knew more than I wanted to as it was. My curiosity would have to remain unsatisfied for now.

"You're pretty awesome," Zeke said suddenly.

I blinked. "I am? Why?"

He smiled. "Because most women would have thrown up, run away or cried. Not you though. You're rattled, but you're not scared. You even came here with me, which shows a shit load of balls. Or to be more accurate, cast iron ovaries."

I felt my face getting hot. It got hotter still when I realised both guys were looking at me with matching expressions of admiration.

"That's pretty badass," Asher agreed. "We've had a lifetime of dealing with this shit, that's the only reason we keep it together."

"Do we keep it together?" Zeke asked.

Asher cocked his head at the lead singer. "I mean, I guess we do. More or less." He made a back and forth gesture with his hand. "We haven't quite come unravelled yet, have we?"

"I suppose not," Zeke conceded. "We might all be badasses."

"I certainly am," Haru remarked. "Now, all of this testosterone is making me twitchy." He made an 'out-out' gesture with his fingers, in the direction of the door.

I couldn't blame him, it was doing the same to me.

I gave Haru a smile and followed the guys back out onto the street.

"Well…" I said awkwardly. "It's been an interesting evening."

"It certainly has." Asher put a hand on the side of my face and leaned in to give me a slow, deep kiss that turned my knees weak. "Good night. Sweet dreams."

In a whisper he added, "Think of me when you're fucking him."

I had no idea how to respond to that. His words and the brush of his breath on my ear made me hot all over. He made it clear he wanted to be with me, but he didn't seem to mind me being with Zeke. Who even were these guys? I didn't know, but shit, I was going to have to stock up on spare panties. Enough for several changes a day.

Before I could, he turned and gave Zeke a quick bro hug.

"Thanks for coming, bro." Zeke patted him on the shoulder then stepped away from him and took my hand.

"We have some unfinished business to attend to."

11

ZEKE

I LED her up to my room and watched her beautiful face as I lay her back on my bed.

I knew she wanted this as much as I did, but the head might have freaked her out more than she was letting on.

It wasn't every day you saw something like that. Unless you worked in a morgue or were Haru. He didn't seem at all fazed by it. I suspected he saw shit like that all the time. I had a funny feeling he actually liked it. He was cool, but strange.

At any rate, Abbie seemed determined to put it all behind her, at least for now. She focused her eyes on mine and started to pull my shirt up and over my head.

I shrugged out of my sleeves and tossed it aside

before I started on her shirt. Her skin was incredible. The more I saw, the more I wanted to see. I wanted to know every freckle, to know the birthmark on her hip by heart. It was shaped like a distorted crescent moon.

Right above that was a tattoo of some kind of flower. I also found a tattoo on her right shoulder, this one of a cat. She also had a different kind of flower on one of her wrists and a treble clef on her ankle.

She had a scar across her abdomen. I traced it with my finger and made a mental note to ask about it later.

In the meantime, I pulled off her skirt and very damp panties and threw them over my shoulder. They landed on my hip before sliding off and onto the floor.

She helped me out of my pants, letting cool air swirl around my hot, hard cock.

I caught her mouth in a deep, searing kiss. Her lips tasted like wine and salt. She smelled of the light perfume she dotted on her neck and throat.

The scent faded into the fresh aroma of soap the further down her body I worked my mouth and hands.

She moaned and writhed as I licked and sucked

her nipples in turn. She was so responsive, she turned me on so fucking hard. Harder enough to hurt, in the best way. My balls ached for her. Begged.

Her little moans and whimpers, shit, I could get used to those. My skin pebbled every time, belly clenching in anticipation.

I worked my way down lower, teasing her belly button with the tip of my tongue. I felt a small circular scar there, like she'd had a navel piercing she let grow out.

I would have to ask her about that too.

I shuffled down lower still until I dipped my head between her legs. I slid an arm under one of her thighs, lifting her ass a little and opening her wider to me.

Slowly, with featherlight touches, I started to explore her pussy with my tongue. She tasted delicious, like sweet butter. The sounds she made when I teased her were more beautiful than music. Her hips moved, trying to push her clit into the path of my touch.

I teased that too, but then moved away to kiss the insides of her thighs.

"Zeke..." she said breathlessly. "Please..."

"Can I play with this?" I ran a finger lightly over her rear hole.

"Mmmm, yeah." She panted out her nose.

"Great." I scooted up and leaned over to the table beside the bed. I opened the drawer and pulled out a narrow, blue vibrator and a tube of lube. I caught her looking at me confused, and grinned before I continued slathering lube all over the vibrator.

I scooted back over and gently bent her legs at her knees, to open her out even more.

Slowly and carefully, with my eyes on her face, I pressed the tip of the vibrator against her rear hole. She tensed and shivered at the shock of the cool toy and lube touching her warm skin.

After a moment she relaxed and looked back at me, a gratifying expression of trust on her face. She knew whatever I did, I would do my best not to hurt her. This was a delicate operation at best, after all.

I licked my lips and pressed the vibrator in a little further. When it was a couple of centimetres in, I pressed the button on the side for a light vibrate. At the same time, I slipped a couple of fingers into her pussy and lowered my mouth back to her clit.

"Oh my God," she breathed.

I smiled to myself and licked her clit and folds lightly while simultaneously pressing my fingers and the vibrator into her. Each thrust got a little deeper, but I glanced at her every few moments to make sure she was okay with all of this.

Honestly, she seemed to be better than okay. Her hips rolled lightly and her hands were tangled in the sheets.

"God, God, God, *fuck...*" She moaned loudly, before her breath turned to a series of whimpers and groans. She ground out the most guttural sound I've ever heard and her muscles tightened around my fingers.

My hand was already damp from her juices, but she wet my fingers even more when she came. And she came hard.

Her back arched and she all but screamed at the ceiling. Her hips bucked and rolled for a minute, two. Just as her body started to still, she cried out again, bucking harder still.

Her second orgasm made my hand wetter than the first. My fingers were more lubricated than the vibrator by now. And I was loving every second of it.

I kept working her in the hope of a third orgasm, but she flopped back down and panted.

I took the hint and slid the vibrator free before I turned it off. I tossed it aside and, slowly and reluctantly, slid my fingers out of her. I could happily have kept them there all day, but my balls would probably burst.

I rolled her over onto her stomach, then carefully guided her up onto all fours in front of me. I was almost a quivering mess of anticipation by now. Making her come was ninety-nine percent of the fun, but I still wanted that one percent.

She looked at me over her shoulder while I positioned my cock outside her pussy. My hands pressed against her stomach, I slid into her slowly.

Fuck. The hot, wet, velvet heat that enveloped my cock was almost enough to make me come immediately. It took a shit load of self-control to keep myself from doing just that.

Not only because I didn't want it over that quickly, but because it would be embarrassing.

What sort of rock god would I be if I couldn't last more than a minute or two? Yeah, okay, one who had a really hot, gorgeous woman around his dick. I was only human after all.

I started to thrust slowly, pulling all the way out and sliding all the way back in, balls deep. When I moved forward, I gradually slid my hands further up her body until I had one of her breasts in each of my hands. Her nipples hardened at my touch. My cock might have hardened a little more too, which I wouldn't have thought was possible.

How did this woman make me feel things no other woman ever had before? There was something about her that drove me crazy.

Crazy in the best way possible.

I couldn't get enough. I wanted to pound her hard and fast and at the same time slowly and for hours.

In the end, she chose the pace. She pushed her hips back against me in an easy, captivating rhythm. I didn't even try to fight her. I closed my eyes and enjoyed her doing her thing, her ass pressing against me every couple of seconds.

"Girl, you're amazing," I said as breathlessly as she had spoken to me earlier.

"Hell yeah I am," she said with laughter in her voice.

I chuckled. I didn't see the point of false modesty, especially when she had no need to be modest. She was sexy, smart and incredible, not to mention she felt really fucking good around my cock.

She started to move faster, driving me closer and closer to spilling myself inside her. I tried with everything in me to make it last as long as possible, but her body drove me wild. Her hips moved faster and I couldn't hold back any longer.

I grunted and gripped her breasts a little harder than I intended as I came, releasing every drop of tension and cum deep into her body. I kept on thrusting, milking myself for every little bit of pleasure. Only when there was nothing left, I sagged, sweating and panting, against her.

She lowered herself back down to the bed, taking me with her. Somehow, I managed to stay inside her for another minute or two, totally unwilling to relinquish the warm space inside her delicious body.

Eventually, I realised I was lying on her and had to slide out and roll off.

"Wow," she said after a few minutes of sleepy silence. "That was... Wow."

"Yeah." I was at least as eloquent as she was. Sometimes there weren't the right words to describe something like this. "Worth waiting for."

"Definitely." She rolled over on her side to face me and smiled softly. "That thing with the vibrator. That was new for me."

"Yeah? You seemed to like it." I gave her a questioning glance.

"I did," she agreed. "I've done anal before, but

never with a vibrator and never with oral at the same time. That made me come so hard."

I leaned in and kissed her nose. "Then I look forward to doing it again. And again. And a bunch of other stuff you might not have ever done before. I'm sure there's plenty you could teach me too."

She smiled softly. "I'm not sure about that, but I'm looking forward to trying."

That was music to my ears. Almost as much as hearing her come. A small part of me half expected her to run out of the room and regret what we did.

Only a small part, though. The rest of me was sure she knew what she was doing and was happy about it as I was.

"I'm sure you're very creative," I assured her. Now I was going to have to be as well. In the meantime, I had to ask.

"Were you thinking of Asher while I was fucking you?" I smiled teasingly.

I couldn't quite make out her blushing, but I was almost sure she was.

"You heard that?" she asked.

I shrugged the shoulder that wasn't pressed against the mattress. "I think that was his intention, but yes I heard. I don't mind if you were. Your body was here with me."

"It certainly was," she said. "My soul might have left my body a couple of times, but my body was here."

"Sorry, not sorry." I grinned. I would never be sorry for making a woman feel good, particularly her.

"You absolutely don't have anything to be sorry about," she said. "I haven't felt so good in…ever."

"Ever?" I said. "That's impressive." I didn't mind being impressed with myself once in a while. Okay, I was often impressed with myself but usually it was about music. Not that I was all that humble about my skills in the bedroom either. But I wouldn't say no to the boost in my ego anyway. An ego could never be too big. Right?

"Just being honest," she said.

She snuggled into me as I pulled the covers over both of us.

"Do me a favour," I said. "Don't ever stop being honest."

"As long as you don't," she said.

"I'll do my best," I assured her. Unless I had to lie to her to keep her safe. I put an arm over her and drew her closer as sleep started to creep up on me. The last thing that crossed my mind before I let it claim me, was that she hadn't told me whether or not she was thinking about Asher.

12

ABBIE

I woke confused but warm. My whole body felt relaxed and satisfied.

It took a couple of languid minutes more to remember why and who I was lying next to.

I rolled onto my side and cracked an eye open.

Zeke was still asleep, his side of the covers half pushed off him.

I had an unimpeded view of his bare torso and chest, tattoos, firm muscles and all. Or should I say tattoo, singular? The ink formed a scene with a wolf in the centre. It stood amongst trees and was surrounded by a variety of animals and mythical creatures. Here and there were symbols I didn't recognise or know the meaning of.

The whole work must have taken hours, and a whole lot of sessions to do.

It was almost as much a work of art as his abs. Without doubt, they also took a lot of work. They were even more impressive than his ink. Maybe it was just my priorities. I loved tattoos, but not as much as muscles.

I thought about licking them, but Zeke opened his eyes and distracted me with his smile.

"Hey beautiful." He stifled a yawn with his hand. "Did you sleep well?"

"Better than I have in years," I said honestly. Usually, I was lucky to get three or four hours of sleep in a row before lying awake for an hour or two. Judging by the light from the window, I'd been out for at least six or seven hours.

"Good." He brushed a kiss over my lips. "I'll be back in a minute." He pushed the covers the rest of the way off and got up.

I admired the view of his tight ass as he headed into the bathroom. Disposing of guns and heads was probably illegal, but his whole body was the real crime here. No one should get away with looking that good.

He glanced out the window on the way back. His whole demeanour changed instantly.

"Fuck."

"What is it?" I pushed myself up on one elbow. "Please tell me it's not another head. Or other body parts." My heart was suddenly racing.

"Oh it's a head all right," he said. "Unfortunately, it's Reuben's head and the rest of him is here too." He stepped over to the wardrobe and started pulling out clothes.

"That's bad, right?" I pushed off the covers and started to gather up my clothes.

He paused for a moment. "Potentially. We should certainly not be naked when I open the door. Although, if you were, that might soften him up a little bit." He grinned to show he was joking.

Playfully, I scooped his pants up off the floor and threw them at his face.

He caught them and laughed. "I assume that's a no." He tossed them aside onto what I assumed was a laundry pile. He pulled on a pair of boxers and dragged track pants up over the top. Not light grey ones, unfortunately.

"I'm going to have a quick shower," I said. "Tell me you're not going to kill each other while I'm in there."

"To the best of my knowledge, Reuben doesn't

want me dead." Zeke pulled a Wolf Venom T-shirt over his head and tugged it down into place.

I had a sneaking suspicion he wore it to goad Reuben. Hopefully that didn't mean things were going to get ugly.

"I hope you're right." I hurried across the corridor to the bathroom.

Before I closed the door, I heard Zeke say, "I hope so too."

This was going to be a lightning quick shower, and getting dressed. I felt uneasy and vulnerable being under the same roof with someone like Reuben Brantley. If he was even half as bad as Zeke said, then I should definitely not turn my back on him, much less be naked around him.

Just in case, I locked the door. Of course, it was the kind of lock you could open with a butter knife, but it made me feel better.

I showered in about two and a half minutes flat, making sure to clean up extra well between my legs. I dried with what I hoped was a clean towel and hurried into my room to get dressed.

From the doorway, I heard male voices talking downstairs. More than two, unless I missed my guess. Who else did Reuben bring with him and what did that mean?

Trouble, presumably.

I stood in front of my wardrobe for a couple of minutes thinking what to wear and ultimately chose a floral sundress that fell to just above my knees. Hopefully it was cute without being provocative.

I dried my hair, tied it back in a ponytail, and applied a tiny splash of make-up.

I pushed my feet into a pair of low heels and, with my heart in my throat, headed down the stairs.

Zeke stood in the kitchen, putting water in the coffee machine.

Three men stood nearby. The two in jeans and plain T-shirts were identical but the resemblance to Zeke was obvious. They were both insanely good-looking in a 'too young for me anyway,' kind of way. Somehow they managed to look menacing and casual at the same time. It was the same vibe, I realised, that Zeke had.

None of them even came close to looking as menacing as the last man. I didn't need anyone to tell me I was looking at Reuben Brantley.

He wore a dark suit and a crisp white button down shirt. He had the kind of face that was hand-some, but at the same time looked like he'd never smiled in his life.

As I reached the bottom of the stairs, he turned

to look at me with blue eyes so piercing I felt like he stripped me naked and whittled away my soul at the same time.

I swallowed in spite of myself. I resolved not to be intimidated, but it was hard not to be in the presence of someone like him.

"Ahhh, there's Abbie," Zeke said. "Coffee is almost ready." He didn't sound anxious, but it was in his body language. He held himself stiffer than usual, tightly coiled, like he was ready to lash out in an instant.

"It sounds like I have good timing then," I said as calmly as I could. I offered Reuben a smile, which he didn't return.

The twins, on the other hand, looked me up and down and grinned.

"She is cute, bro," one of them said. He stepped over to me and held out his hand. "I'm Parker. I'm sure Zeke has told you a lot about me. It's probably all true. If you get tired of him, look me up. Twins are much more fun. Right, Hunter?"

"He's not wrong," Hunter said. He gave me a smile that might have been seductive if I didn't have his brother to compare him to.

They were adorable, but they were Zeke two-point-oh at best. A thought I would be better off keeping to myself.

"That's Reuben," Parker said helpfully. He jerked his head towards his other brother. "Before you ask, yes he was born with that cranky expression on his face. Some of us think it was tattooed on."

Reuben's expression didn't change except a narrowing of his eyes at his youngest brother.

"I'm sure having six younger brothers would make anyone cranky," I said lightly.

Now he turned his ice cold gaze onto me. I wished I hadn't spoken.

"That depends on the brothers," he said, his voice a deep rumble. "Some are easier to deal with than others." He didn't have to look at Zeke for everyone in the room to know who he was talking about.

"Ain't that the truth?" Zeke said. He shot Reuben a sarcastic smile.

Reuben looked even less impressed than he had already. "You're the one who contacted me. Have you decided to give up on playing around at being a musician?" He talked about it like he couldn't think of a less worthy profession for his brother than that. Or a less serious one.

"No," Zeke said lightly. He pulled coffee cups out

of the cupboard and placed them on the bench near the coffee machine. "I thought I'd give it a go for a little while longer. I have a feeling we'll be successful any day now." He turned away to start pouring coffee.

One of the twins chuckled, but I couldn't tell if it was Parker or Hunter. Either way, they fell silent after a glance from Reuben. Presumably, they were the dutiful brothers, even though they pushed the envelope a little bit. Evidently laughing at Zeke's comment was a step too far. Or at least half a step.

"What is this about?" Reuben demanded. "I haven't come here so you could waste my time."

Parker opened his mouth to say something, but snapped it shut again. Judging by the look in his eyes, he had a smartass comment on his lips. It was probably better if he didn't provoke his brother any further.

"Jonah is dead," Zeke said over his shoulder. He turned around, cup in hand and offered it to Reuben. "Milk?"

Reuben looked at him like he'd grown a second or third head. "You killed him?"

"No," Zeke said quickly. He put the cup down near Reuben so he could get it himself, and explained about the present on the doorstep the night before.

"Did you have him killed because he didn't get me to come back into the fold?"

"No," Reuben snapped. "Suspicions on who did?"

If I thought he looked pissed when I first saw him, it was nothing to how he looked now.

It wasn't the same simmering rage Penn had. It was a cool fury that bubbled below the surface. He was contained, more than anyone I ever met.

I suspected that was part of what made him so dangerous. He was very much in control of himself and—presumably—the people around him most of the time.

Zeke shrugged and took a sip of coffee. "Not a clue. I could guess all day and not get it right. You? Any ideas?"

"If I knew, they would be dead right now," Reuben said. He glanced at me but didn't look even slightly sorry for speaking so frankly.

I wondered if he was worried I would go to the police. I quickly realised how silly that thought was.

He knew I knew about the head and I hadn't said anything. That made me an accessory. Further, if his reach was anywhere near what Zeke implied it was, I would be dead before I found a cop who would listen to me. I was in this even deeper than ever.

Oh, goody.

"Did you have to get rid of his head before we got to see it?" Hunter complained.

I raised an eyebrow at him.

He shrugged. "Just to prove it was really Jonah."

I didn't think that was it at all, but whatever. He wouldn't be the first person on the face of the planet to be bloodthirsty, and he wouldn't be the last.

I mean, someone cut off the guy's head. That was pretty fucking bloodthirsty right there.

"It was Jonah," Zeke said. "I wouldn't have you standing in my kitchen if it wasn't."

"I thought it was because you love us." Parker pouted.

Zeke snorted.

"Ouch." Parker raised his hand as though to flip Zeke off but then he glanced at Reuben and lowered his hand.

They certainly had an interesting family dynamic. Reuben had them on a leash, but not necessarily a tight one. Or maybe it wasn't as tight as he would like it to be.

Were the twins trying to rebel the way Zeke was? I'd like to think Zeke would help them if they did, but there didn't seem to be much love lost between them and him.

I wondered about his other brothers. Was he

close to any of them at all, or was Wolf Venom more of a family to him then they were?

"We'll be going." Reuben nodded to the twins, gave Zeke a long, intense glare, then headed towards the door.

"Nice talk," Zeke said. He watched them leave, his body tense until the door closed behind them.

13

ABBIE

"So you met Reuben?" Tully looked sympathetic.

"Yeah, he seems charming," I said sarcastically. I looked across the rehearsal room to where Zeke sat talking to Asher. They spoke too softly for me to hear, but Zeke's expression was grim. It had been since his brother left the townhouse.

Tully sat down beside me, almost close enough to touch. "He's always like that just after he's seen any of his brothers. He'll bounce back in an hour or two. He always does."

I turned my head to take a good look at him. Like the other guys, he was ridiculously attractive. He and Channing seemed to be the serious ones of the group for most part.

Right now, Tully's wide mouth was turned up in

a slight smile. His eyes, which looked like liquid chocolate, caught me in their gaze.

Where I felt like Reuben tried to eviscerate my soul, it seemed like Tully was trying to see into my mind and heart. I wasn't sure he would like what he found in there either, but it was hard to look away.

"You know all about his family?" I asked, to distract from the moment. "Are you okay with it?"

He pressed the pad of his thumb to his lower lip and considered that question for a moment.

"I'm not okay with them, as such, but I'm more than okay with Zeke. He's not his family. He's tried for a long time to get away from them and put their bullshit behind him. It's hard when you live your life as visibly as we do. He could have disappeared a long time ago if he was—I don't know—a plumber."

"I can't imagine him fixing toilets." I picked up a bottle of water from the floor beside my chair and opened it to take a sip.

Tully chuckled. "Neither can I. I think he was always meant to do something in the public eye."

"That must make it difficult to be a shady person," I said slowly. "People always want to know about our families for some reason. I can't imagine Reuben liking that kind of attention on him or his dealings."

"Most of the world thinks of him as a legitimate

businessman," Tully explained. "Having Zeke in the spotlight has probably made him a lot of money."

"Then why not let him keep being in the spotlight?" I asked. Making more money was good motivation for a lot of people.

"Because Reuben values obedience over pretty much everything else." Tully shifted in his seat so the side of his arm touched the side of mine.

I didn't know if he did it on purpose or by accident, but that slight touch was like a charge of electricity all the way through me. I remembered what Zeke said about all the guys wanting to do naughty things with me.

I was starting to want to do naughty things with them too.

"Even money?" It was a little harder to think, but I managed to speak coherently.

"I don't know for sure, but I suspect he has so much money he doesn't need to worry about it too much." The look in Tully's eyes suggested he knew he was getting to me and that the feeling was mutual.

I hadn't anticipated any of this when the label paired me with Wolf Venom. Honestly, all I thought about was getting my career back on track. I knew who they were, I knew their music, but I hadn't thought about connecting with any of them.

It was possible they saw me as fresh meat or something like that, but I didn't think so.

Zeke, Asher and Tully at least seemed to see me as a person. I hadn't had much time to talk to Landon or Channing yet, and Penn was...Penn.

I didn't think he would ever see me as anything but a pain in his ass.

That line of thought brought me back to Zeke and the vibrator and then for some reason I was wondering where Penn would have put it on me, or in me. Thinking like that was unlikely to get me anywhere but frustrated. It wasn't like I was going to find out anyway.

Maybe.

"What about you?" I asked. "What's your family like?"

"Pretty ordinary," he said. "I grew up in the suburbs. One sister, one dog, one cat. Several gold-fish. Mum was a teacher, Dad was an accountant. Pretty boring compared to some of the other guys." He nodded towards Zeke and Asher.

"That sounds nice," I said. "Sometimes boring is safer and easier."

"And sometimes it leads you to rebel and join a

rock band." He grinned and his mouth looked wider still. I couldn't remember having ever seen anyone with such a big, beautiful smile. It was impossible not to smile back.

"Is that what you did?" I asked. "What do your parents think of that?"

His smile faded and for a moment I thought he was going to say they didn't approve.

Instead he said, "They love it. Apparently I'm not good at rebelling."

He spoke so deadpan I didn't realise he was joking at first. When I did, I laughed.

"What a disappointment," I said. "What could you have done that would have pissed them off?"

"I don't know," he admitted. "I could have gone into politics. Then again, they'd expect me to change the world so they wouldn't be disappointed. Until I failed."

"Was that ever on the cards?" I asked.

"Fuck no," he said firmly. "I'd sooner work for the Brantley family, although they're nuts. Zeke is the only one of them who is close to being sane and, well, that is a low bar. Same with Asher's family. And Penn's, but in a different way."

"Oh?" I was as curious about his as I was about any of the other guys' families. It sounded like Penn came from a privileged background. It figured he turned out a spoiled brat.

"Are we going to rehearse or what?" As if he knew we were talking about him, Penn stood and moved over to his keyboard.

"Yes, we are," Zeke agreed. Whatever Asher said to him, he seemed a lot happier than he'd been all morning. The two guys seem to be closer with each other than with the other guys in the band. Not as close as Landon and Channing, as far as I could tell, but good friends anyway.

"That's our cue." Tully stood and offered me his hand to stand.

I took it and rose. I wasn't even surprised when he didn't let it go until he led me over to my mic stand.

No one else looked surprised either but, predictably, Penn looked pissed.

I sincerely hoped he would get over himself at some point. I didn't know if anything more would develop with any of the guys, but he wasn't going to get rid of me as easily as he might hope. If he didn't like that, too fucking bad. I didn't want to cause trouble between him and any of his bandmates, but I wasn't going to let him stop me from living my life.

"Abbie and I talked about it and we think she

should join us on 'Before I Stay' and 'Someone I'm Over,'" Zeke said. "Any objections?"

"Works for me," Landon said with an easy smile.

"Yeah, all good." Channing shrugged indifferently.

"Let's do it." Asher flashed me a grin that made my pulse speed up.

Penn grunted, which everyone, including me, ignored. If he objected, he was outnumbered anyway.

"Sounds good." Tully stepped away from me and swung his guitar strap over his shoulder.

"Good." Zeke snaked an arm around my waist. "Come on then, you motherfuckers, let's make some music!"

I pulled my mic out of the stand and brought it to my lips.

"Let's make—" I lowered the microphone and turned it on before I tried again. "Let's make beautiful music."

The guys laughed but they were laughing *with* me and not *at* me. I couldn't bring myself to look at Penn, just in case.

Zeke grinned and turned on his mic. He turned to Asher and nodded.

The drummer nodded back and started the beat for the first song.

Landon, on his bass, was right there with him. The others, like a well oiled machine, slipped in effortlessly.

Zeke and I raised our mics and locked eyes on each other. I knew the song well enough to know when to come in, but my heart raced like crazy. It always did before any kind of performance, but this was different. I didn't want to screw this up. For so very many reasons, including not wanting the guys pissed at me. They needed to know that when we stepped out on stage, I wasn't going to make them look bad.

Doubt crept into my mind. What if I messed up? What if I made a complete fool of myself? I could get out there and forget all the lyrics. Or I could come in at the wrong time. Or I could fall on my face, literally. Or I could just sound bad.

Apparently Zeke could tell I was psyching myself out, big time. He gave me a reassuring smile and hugged me a little tighter.

That was all I needed. When it came time to sing, the words came out in near perfect unison with Zeke's. Getting it exactly right was going to take practice, but we sounded pretty damn good together. Our voices were the perfect blend of his deep, gravelly masculine, and my lighter tone.

By the time we finished the first chorus, I knew we chose the right song to sing. Hopefully the label and Jackson would agree. I had a feeling Zeke had a lot of sway with both of them. Certainly a shit load more than I did. I would have to go along with whatever they decided and keep smiling like I loved the idea, even if I didn't.

Curious, I turned to see what the other guys thought. I got the impression they liked it. Certainly none of them looked like they hated it.

Every one of them seemed laid-back and relaxed. In their groove. They would have played this song a billion times before, so they could do it in their sleep. Even with a new voice added to the mix. It would take more than that to throw them off.

They all made playing their instrument look easy, which I knew none of them were. Especially at their level of skill. I could play guitar and piano, but nowhere near as well as these guys.

There was something especially thrilling about singing with other professionals like this. Not just because they were hot, but because they loved what they did and they did it well. Even if you didn't like their kind of music, you would have to appreciate their ability.

Asher grinned at me without faltering for a moment. He looked like he was having the time of his life behind his drums. He probably was.

When my gaze went to Tully, he gave me a wink. I wasn't sure whether or not making the guitar cry right now was part of the song, but he did it anyway and it totally worked.

I smiled around my microphone and turned back to Zeke. Just like the others, he looked like he was having too much fun. He certainly looked a lot happier than he had an hour ago.

I totally got that. Music was the perfect place to escape to when life got rough. It was like a blanket fort full of chocolate and wine, and a pile of good books. Okay, those things were pretty good too, but music was my life. Spending the last year without being able to perform, was a special kind of hell. One I didn't want to revisit.

The idea of going back there was much scarier than Reuben, a gun or a disembodied head.

14

ZEKE

"No more heads turned up?" Asher asked. He leaned his shoulder against the wall beside me and crossed his arms over his chest.

"Not yet," I said. "Everything is eerily quiet. No one has waved a gun at me and I haven't heard from any of my brothers."

He frowned. "You think they're up to something?"

"When are they not?" I idly ran the tip of my finger around the Wolf Venom logo on the side of one of my headphones. The label had them made especially for us. They even let us choose our own individual colours. Apart from the logo, mine were black.

"It was annoying as shit when they were threatening me and nagging me to come back to the family, but I knew what was going on. This silence is freaky as fuck."

They were planning something. They had to be. Reuben didn't leave anything alone, particularly after one of his men was killed.

In spite of me telling him I wasn't involved, I couldn't rule out the possibility he thought I was. After all, it was my doorstep. And my head Jonah waved the gun at. And Abbie's, which was even worse.

I didn't like being threatened, but the thought of anything happening to her made my blood boil. If anyone tried, I might rip their head off. Not necessarily the one on their shoulders either.

I realised I was gripping my headphones so hard my hand was white. I loosened my grip before I broke them. Levi might be pissed if he had to fork out for replacements too often.

"They might not be up to anything at all," Asher said reasonably.

I snorted and raised my eyebrows at him. "You have met these people, right? If they aren't up to something, then they're probably dead."

"That's a possibility," Asher said. "Maybe somebody went after Jonah and then went after them." He tilted his head questioningly. "According to rumours, the Fiorellis are getting restless."

"We would have heard about it by now." I hated to admit it, but a small part of me wished that was true. They were my family, and I cared about them in a dutiful brother kind of way, but they wouldn't expect me to return to the family if there wasn't a family to return to.

Reuben's enemies would rejoice if he was out of the way. Until someone came along to fill the void. And they would. It was as inevitable as dog crap. Someone was always ready to step up and take their place.

"I guess so," Asher agreed. "Probably just as well, They wouldn't stop until they got the rest of us."

"Or the rest of the Brantley family anyway," I said. "The rest would depend on whether or not they decided to take out the DiMarcos while they were there." We talked about it all so casually, but the carnage would be horrific. Without doubt, innocent people would be caught up, not just us.

Asher grimaced. "I don't know why they'd bother. It's not like we have any power or influence anymore."

"You have plenty of influence," I reminded him.

"If you wear a bright green T-shirt, bright green T-shirts suddenly get really popular."

He chuckled. "Oh good, I'm a fashionista." He pretended to fluff his hair. "At least that kind of influence is mostly harmless."

"Mostly being the key word." I looked up as Jackson walked past the room. "What is taking so long?"

"You have somewhere better to be?" Asher asked.

"Better than in the studio listening to our new album to make sure it's as awesome as we want to be? Between that and taking Abbie to lunch, it's a tie."

I wanted her to be here with us today, but the label insisted on sorting out her wardrobe for the upcoming tour. Apparently her performing naked was out of the question, worse luck.

It would be very distracting for all of us if she did, but a guy could wish, right?

Asher smiled. "She's pretty amazing, isn't she?"

I raised an eyebrow at him. "If I didn't know better, I'd think you are smitten."

"Aren't you?" he countered.

I thought about denying it, but I grinned in spite of myself. "I guess you could say that. Do we have a problem here?"

"What? Do you want me to fight you for her?" He raised his fists as if he might actually try to punch me out, but he had the goofiest expression on his face.

I barked a laugh. "First of all, I would whoop your ass and you know it. Second of all, it's my house she's staying in." If I had my way, that wouldn't change.

"And third, if she wants you instead of me, then that's up to her."

"What if she wants you as *well* as me?" Asher asked. "What if she wants all of us?"

I saw her look at Tully with the same interest she showed me and Asher. I'd also seen her cast speculative looks in Landon and Channing's direction.

Penn, she regarded with a combination of curiosity and animosity.

"As long as she's happy, then I'm down with it," I said finally. We shared a buttload of other things, why not a woman? Honestly, I'd rather share her than not have her at all.

I guessed that meant I was more than smitten. If she was anyone else, that would have freaked me the fuck out. With her, I was one hundred percent here for it.

"So it won't bother you if I ask her out?" Asher asked.

"It will bother me while there's someone out there cutting off heads and putting them in boxes," I said. "I don't even like letting her out of my sight for this long. Otherwise, no, it wouldn't bother me. She's free to see whoever she wants."

"Are you?" he gave me a questioning look again.

"Am I what?" I frowned at him.

"Are you free to see anyone you like?"

I opened my mouth to say of course I was, but that wasn't what came out.

"I don't want to see anyone else." I really didn't. No other woman even came close to her. Even thinking about it felt like cheating.

God, when did this happen? Whatever, I wasn't even mad about it.

"Neither do I," Asher admitted. "She really is something else, isn't she?"

"She totally is." I looked up as Jackson stopped in the doorway and gestured towards us.

"You're up," he said.

I nodded and stood. "I feel like this should be weird," I said to Asher. "Is it weird that it isn't weird?"

"No, it just proves that we're even more awesome than we already thought we were." He grinned.

"Huh. I wouldn't have thought that was possible." I chuckled. We were pretty amazing, and none of us were particularly modest, not even me.

"I know. I am amazed." Asher stepped out the door ahead of me.

"What are you amazed by?" Landon asked. As usual, he and Channing were virtually joined at the hip.

"Our own maturity," I said. "And the fact we both like Abbie enough to share her with whoever else she wants to be with."

"Interesting," Tully said from behind them. "Does she know any of this?"

"You're all fucking insane," Penn snapped. "We've known her for all of about five minutes and we're ready to share her around like she's a pizza."

"She's better than pizza," I said. "The point is, a few of us like her and we're not going to punch each other out over it. Aren't you proud of us?"

He gave me a look like I was speaking a different language. "After the tour, none of us will ever see her again."

"First of all, I'm going to make sure that's not the case," I said slowly. "Just because you don't like her doesn't mean the rest of us can't."

"He did include himself in 'we,'" Asher pointed out.

All of us turned to look at Penn.

"He did, didn't he?" I said.

"Fuck off," Penn said. "It was a slip of the tongue. And also accurate. We—" he emphasised the word "—have known her for about five minutes. Just because I'm a part of this band doesn't mean I give a crap about her." Like usual, he scowled.

"It doesn't mean you don't," I said. "There's nothing wrong with liking someone. Especially someone as—"

He stopped mid-step, turned and got almost chest-to-chest with me. "I. Don't. Like. Her. Get the fuck over it. The sooner the better." He pushed past me and stomped off down the corridor after Jackson.

"I've heard hate fucking is good," I called out after him.

He flipped with me off with a finger over his shoulder.

I chuckled. "Does that sound like a man who isn't interested to you guys?"

"Maybe you shouldn't push it any further," Tully said softly. Always the voice of reason. "Just because we all seem to like her, doesn't mean she feels the same way. Chances are she would only choose one of us anyway. At the end of the day, this conversation is probably all for nothing."

Asher and I sighed.

"Tully is right," Asher said. "She might have chosen already. After all, she is living in Zeke's house."

While I didn't mind sharing, I also didn't mind *not* sharing.

"I'll talk to her," I said. "See where her head is at. Don't be surprised if her answer is that she's thinking about the tour."

"We should all be doing that," Channing said. "Whatever happens will happen. I for one I'm happy to roll with it. Right Landon?"

"Right." Landon nodded and leaned over to give Channing a quick kiss on the mouth. "Rolling with it works for me."

They really were way too cute together.

"If you guys don't hurry up, you don't get to have any say in how well the songs were mixed," Jackson said, sticking his head out the doorway.

"Pig's ass. As if you're going to start without us." I laughed.

He grimaced and rolled his eyes. "Maybe not," he

agreed. "But we might take the cost of the time you're taking out of your royalties."

Considering we wouldn't notice the shortfall, we all laughed. We didn't even walk faster. We were Wolf Venom, or as our fans referred to us, The Venom. Our producer and manager would wait for us for as long as it took. What was the point of being a rock god if you couldn't push the envelope? At the end of the day, they worked for us. The label wasn't going to drop us anytime soon, we made them way too much money.

I stepped into the studio and pushed my earpieces in. They were connected via bluetooth to the producer's console. The studio had headsets, but I preferred my own.

My idea of sharing didn't include earwax. Sweat, cum, lube, saliva, sure, but not earwax.

I wondered what Abbie would think about the conversation we just had. There was a distinct possibility she would think we were completely crazy.

I knew she wasn't only interested in me, but did that go beyond sex? What if I talked to her and she said it didn't? It wouldn't change how I felt about her and it certainly wouldn't stop me from fucking her.

The only thing that would stop me from doing that was her.

I wasn't wrong when I said we should focus on the album and the tour. Was now a good time to complicate things further?

Yeah, okay, on some level, I was trying to talk myself out of speaking to her because I wasn't sure what she'd say. My ego wasn't fragile, but I wanted her in my life more than I wanted anything else. If things got ugly between us, it would make the tour difficult for everyone. Levi might even pull her from it, to get her out of my hair.

The solution to that was easy. I wouldn't let things get ugly. The best way I knew to do that was with food, wine and orgasms.

Lots and lots of orgasms.

15

ABBIE

"YOU LOOK BEAUTIFUL," Landon said softly, his mouth near my ear.

"What he said," Channing said as he slipped up behind us.

"You too," I said without thinking. My face heated. "I mean, you both look handsome."

The three of us hung back behind the rest of Wolf Venom. Both guys seemed happy to let the others bask in the limelight.

As for me, this was *their* album launch party. I was only here at the insistence of the guys and White Wolf Records.

I tried to argue that I might detract from the real celebration, but they insisted. The label even paid for the dress I wore.

Black and glittering with sequins, the dress was high at the front but plunged almost to the top of my panties at the back. A slit in the side revealed most of my left leg. My updo and make-up were done to perfection. I couldn't remember the last time I got all dressed up like this.

I felt sexy, but self-conscious as hell.

Okay, a lot of that was down to the media with their cameras and questions. So far, they were throwing them at the guys and asking them to stop for photos. Sooner or later, someone would notice—

I hadn't even finished that thought when someone shouted, "Abbie Hart! Can you tell us how it feels to be signed with a new label?"

I wanted to ignore them and hurry past into the party. Instead, I gave them a fake smile and said, "It feels good."

I moved on a few steps before another shouted.

"Abbie, what do you think about Vance getting engaged after your short marriage?"

I almost tripped over nothing, but Landon grabbed my elbow and saved me from falling.

I gave him a quick smile of gratitude. This was the first I'd heard of the asshole with anyone else. If anyone deserved to be a disembodied head, it was Vance.

I flashed another fake smile. "I wish him luck and happiness." I hoped whoever they were, they treated him the same way he treated me. Or worse. Worse was good.

"Abbie, do you think you'll be successful in reviving your career after all the scandals?" That was from Poppy Newton, a tabloid journalist who seemed to have a particular dislike for me.

The feeling was mutual.

To her, I gave the nastiest smile of all.

"Of course I do, Poppy. You know what they say about there being no such thing as bad publicity."

She gave me a similar smile in return. "Are you saying those scandals were nothing but publicity stunts aimed at furthering your career?"

I wanted to remind her she made a career out of reporting this shit to a public hungry for stuff that was none of their business. If anyone was fuelling misery for people like me, it was people like her.

In the corner of my eye, I caught Penn watching the conversation. I hoped like hell he'd keep his mouth closed for once. If he made a comment like he usually did, it might make the situation a hundred times worse. And we both knew it.

I wanted to groan out loud at the idea.

A media shitstorm could make a lot of extra

publicity for the tour, but it could also get me kicked off it.

It was all too ironic, considering his colourful past. Which, I noticed, no one asked him about. Maybe they were told that subject was off-limits.

Past Penn, I saw Zeke, Asher and Tully all looking irritated. The smile I gave them was sincere. This was nothing I couldn't handle. I'd spent the last couple of years fielding bullshit questions like this.

"Come on Poppy," I said smoothly. "We both know if I was going to do something for publicity, it would be much more original than getting married for a few hours. It was just one of those things. Sometimes people are impetuous and jump in before they take a good look at the water." Sometimes the water was full of sharks, or pollution.

"Are you sleeping with Zeke Brantley?" Poppy shot off the question so quickly, it was clearly designed to catch me by surprise.

That was exactly what it did. I tried to stammer out a denial, but it wouldn't come.

"I don't see what that's got to do with anything," I said finally.

"It would explain why you're going on tour with Wolf Venom," she said with barely contained delight. She obviously thought she was onto a big story here.

Or at least, another opportunity to make me look like a desperate, washed up artist.

I didn't think she'd be happy until my career was over. Bitch.

"The fact that she's talented is why she is going on tour with Wolf Venom." It was Jackson who stepped in to respond to that particular accusation. "Her private life is no one's business but hers. Now, if you'll excuse us, we have a party to get to."

Poppy looked like he'd given her a lemon to suck, but she smiled insincerely and stepped back.

"Thank you," I said softly as I walked beside the band's manager to the door of the club.

Landon and Channing jostled for position on the other side of me. Both looked like they wished they'd stepped in to help me out. Honestly, it was better that they didn't. That might have created more questions I didn't want to have to answer.

"You're welcome," Jackson said. "Like I said before, you're part of the family now. I don't like a member of the family getting attacked by rabid chihuahuas like her." After a moment, he reluctantly added, "She's probably going to publish that anyway."

I sighed. "I know. People like her can't help themselves." There were a lot of worse things to talk about than whether or not I was sleeping with Zeke, so I was probably getting off lightly. A severed head would be a much bigger story and create a shit load of problems for all of us.

"I think you handled it well," Zeke said, his eyes full of approval and—was that affection? "I would have said yes and told her to piss off." He glanced back out the door in the direction of Poppy.

"Yeah, but you have no shame." Asher grinned.

Zeke managed to squeeze in beside me and take my hand. "I have nothing to be ashamed of. And neither does Abbie." He leaned in and whispered in my ear, "Do you want me to have her killed for you? Because I could."

I wasn't sure if he was joking or not, but I shook my head. "As tempting as that is, I wouldn't want you to get into trouble for me."

He nibbled my ear for a moment and said, "Okay. Let me know if you change your mind."

I shivered with the delicious sensations his touch sent through my body. "I'll bear that in mind."

"I'm happy to make the same offer," Asher said.

When I turned to look at him questioningly, he grinned. "I'm guessing he offered to have her taken care of, because I was about to do the same thing."

I shook my head at them both. For guys who said

they wanted to get away from their families and the violence they were involved in, they were quick enough to offer their families' contacts to deal with a problem. I couldn't decide if that was terrifying or sexy as hell.

Maybe all of the above.

"Can we forget about it and enjoy ourselves?" Tully stepped up behind me and to my surprise, slipped his arms around my waist. "Would you like a drink? Or a dance?"

I leaned back and looked at him over my shoulder. "Both?"

"What the woman wants, the woman gets," he said. Apparently the party atmosphere brought out his flirty side. I liked it. It was nice to see him relax a little bit.

When Zeke let my hand go, Tully took it and led me over to the bar.

"Drinks are on the label tonight," he said with a smile.

"I'll drink to that." I ordered a glass of champagne and toasted Tully with it. He toasted me back with his glass of beer.

We took a few sips and moved to the dance floor.

While I grooved carefully, and tried not to spill

my drink, I glanced around and tried not to gawk like a starstruck teenager.

The guest list was a who's who of the music industry. Not just in Australia; a lot of international faces were here tonight as well. Producers, artists, executives for various labels, they all turned up to rub elbows with each other.

Several famous actors were here tonight as well. I recognised one of the world's most popular Australian action heroes standing off to the side with his equally gorgeous and talented wife.

Events like this always made me feel like I was a nobody. Hell, they probably made the guys feel like they were nobodies, and this was *their* party.

"It's surreal, isn't it?" Tully asked, as if he read my mind. "Everywhere I turn, I see someone I recognise. Someone whose music I have on my playlist. Someone I'd love to work with. I'd love to try my hand at acting some day, but who knows if I'd be any good at it?" He shrugged as though he wasn't too worried either way. It wasn't like he needed to succeed at it to put food on his table.

"I'm sure you'd be amazing," I said firmly. "What are music videos if they aren't acting?"

Apart from being really uncomfortable to make. They were definitely not the highlight of my career, especially the lip synching. I'd prefer to do just about anything else. They were an evil necessity though, unfortunately.

"True," he said reflectively. "After the tour, I might look around for an opportunity. You never know, I might be the next big silver screen hero."

I smiled. "I would come and see your movies. I know the rest of the guys would too."

"They better," he growled playfully. "I know where they all live."

I laughed, drank down the rest of my champagne and handed my glass to a passing server.

"You're making threats now?" I asked. Without a drink in my hand, I was able to move closer and put my hand lightly on his shoulder.

He took my hand and put his other one on my hip. It wasn't exactly the right kind of music for a slow dance position, but whatever. Neither of us cared.

He pressed the length of his body against mine and spoke in my ear. "I don't make threats, I make promises."

We both laughed.

In the back of my mind, I wondered if maybe he was involved in the same things as Zeke and Asher and their families, but downplayed it more than they did. He said he had a quiet, suburban upbringing, but that didn't mean he wasn't in it as deep.

I knew them for only a couple of weeks, and already I saw much more than I would ever have dreamed of seeing. Tully had known them for years and was fully aware of their pasts. I could only guess at the things he might have seen and done.

What about the rest of the guys then? It wasn't too much of a stretch to think Penn was involved in things he shouldn't be. He oozed rebel bad boy, as well as asshole.

Landon and Channing—they both seemed more innocent than the rest of the guys, but I knew as well as anyone that there was no guarantee of anything. They could be cat burglars or counterfeiters for all I knew. For the thrill, of course. Neither needed the money.

Jackson, now that I thought about it, probably knew the same things the rest of the guys did. How far up the label did it go? Did Levi Jones have any idea?

I had a feeling he must. A guy like him was too savvy not to know everything that went on in his business.

Before I completely lost my mind in speculation, Tully interrupted my thoughts and leaned in to kiss me. His mouth was rough on mine, contradicting his calm, controlled exterior. It sent a spike of desire right to my pussy.

I had a feeling if we weren't in a room full of people, he would have pushed me hard up against a wall and pounded into me until I screamed with pain and pleasure.

Yeah, he conveyed all of that with one kiss.

Holy shit.

By the time we broke apart, I was panting and yet another pair of panties was ruined.

These guys.

16

ABBIE

AFTER THAT KISS, I danced with most of the guys—not Penn—and a few other guys who asked. Most of them were people I knew or had worked with in the past. A couple I recognised but hadn't met before.

Judging by the looks they gave me and the way they tried to touch my ass on and off the dance floor, they hoped I'd go home with them at the end of the night. My reputation didn't matter to them, they just wanted a fuck.

The only person I went home with was Zeke. My mind buzzed with questions and alcohol. A potentially dangerous combination at the best of times.

He held my hand while we walked up to the townhouse. In spite of the vibe between us, that was all we did. No kissing or undressing each other in the street.

Considering we found the head the last time we came home after an evening out, a bit of caution was understandable.

"No cardboard box," he remarked when we got close enough to see the front steps.

"Fuck yeah," I said. "No random feet that aren't attached to legs either."

"No hands. But most of all, no disembodied cock or ass." He swung our hands between us.

"Thank God for that." Those might be worse than seeing a head.

Maybe.

I didn't know.

They all sounded awful.

"No Reuben waiting outside for us and glaring," he added to the growing list.

"No Poppy Newton hiding in the bushes with her camera." I glanced around to make sure. If she was hiding in the shadows, I couldn't see her.

"Shame." He grinned, teeth flashing white in the streetlight. "We could have given her a show."

He must have decided it was safe, because he pressed me against the door and slanted his mouth over mine. He kissed me, possessive and demanding.

His hands wandered up my arms, to my shoulders. He tangled his fingers in the straps of my dress before tugging them to either side.

The dress slid down my legs and pooled at my feet. I stood in front of him wearing only a black G-string and sequined black stiletto heels.

"That's better. I thought you were overdressed. You looked beautiful, but I much prefer you this way." He bent forward to flick his tongue over one of my nipples. While he did that, he slid his thumbs into the sides of my panties and pushed them down until they joined my dress on the ground.

Except for my heels, I was completely naked for anyone walking past to see. And I didn't even care.

I cared even less when he knelt down in front of me and gently pried my legs apart. He bent one of my knees enough so he could slowly start to devour my pussy with his mouth and tongue.

I pressed my hands against the door and leaned my head back, eyes closed in enjoyment. He nipped at my folds and lapped at my entrance before sucking on my clit.

My hands curled into fists as desire rose. It rushed up like a tsunami, threatening to wash me away and shatter me into a million pieces.

I couldn't hold back a moan that was so loud the

neighbours probably heard. Whatever. Let them hear. Hell, let them come out and watch.

I was vaguely aware of someone walking past who stopped to do just that before they hurried on. I hoped they enjoyed the show. I also hoped they didn't video it, because that bullshit would go viral and I would be fucked in more ways than one.

Luckily it was too dark in front of the door for them to see my face clearly.

"Maybe we should take this inside," I said with what little breath I had to speak. That was followed by another moan as he pressed his fingers inside me. He curled them around to massage my G spot, while not letting up on my clit for a moment.

Or I could just come out here.

I cracked my eyes open at the sound of footsteps which stopped nearby. A couple of guys stood near the gate, watching. The polite thing to do would have been to smile, but I came instead.

I gasped out loud and bucked my hips against Zeke's mouth and hand. The whole world disappeared in an explosion of stars, fireworks and maybe a rainbow or two.

Knowing people were watching made it even more intense and exciting.

Finally, I came down with a whimper and a racing pulse.

The guys actually clapped.

I gave a half bow and a choking laugh before they moved on.

Zeke slipped a shining hand out of me and stood, a grin on his face. "Seems like we put on quite the performance."

"Apparently," I agreed. "Let's take this inside. I have an idea." I bent to pick up my dress and panties.

"Should I be scared?" He didn't look at all scared or even worried. That was good, he had no need to be.

"You'll be fine," I said lightly. I waited until he unlocked the door and went upstairs with him to his room. I tossed my clothes aside and helped him to get out of his.

"I assume you washed that vibrator?" I put my hand on his chest and shoved him back on the bed.

"Of course I did." He rolled over and pulled it out of the drawer along with the lube. "You want me to use it on you again?"

I took both from him. "Not exactly. I figured it might be fun to see how it feels to do that to someone else. If you're game?"

His eyes widened and for a moment he looked a little nervous. "Um."

The bed dipped as I sat down beside him. "You don't have to if you don't want to. There's plenty of other things we could do." I could have made him do it if I wanted to, but I was all about consent.

"No, I do," he said quickly. "You just took me by surprise. I expected…I dunno, anything but that."

His eyes flicked to me, more tentative than I'd seen him before, but willing. "Promise to be gentle? I haven't done anything like this before."

"Of course I will." I hadn't done it to anyone either, and I was scared of hurting him. If anything, I'd be too gentle. I'd watch him and let him guide me. And be ready to stop the second he gave any sign of discomfort.

I applied a literal load of lube to the vibrator and put the tube aside.

Eyes on his face I bent his knees and turned the vibrator on to a low hum. I curled one hand around the base of his already erect cock and licked his tip.

I teased him like that for a while before I closed my lips around him and started to suck.

He groaned and closed his eyes. "Hell yeah, your mouth is fucking incredible."

When his body started to move with me, I slid

the vibrator lightly over his balls before I pressed the very tip of the into his rear hole. It wasn't more than half a centimetre for now.

I glanced up to see his eyelids flutter, but his eyes stayed closed.

Encouraged, I pushed it in a little further. I didn't want to rush this. Anal wasn't something to be jumped into too hard and fast, so to speak.

I lifted my mouth off him long enough to ask, "Is that okay?"

"Mmmm. Hell yeah. That's…different, but I like it."

"Let me know if it doesn't feel good and I'll stop." I lowered my mouth to his cock and went back to sucking. Like he had done with me, I got into a rhythm of sucking and thrusting gently.

I only put the vibrator in a centimetre or two in. Later, if he wanted to try this again, I would see how far he could take it.

I admit, I hoped I'd get to find out. It was refreshing to be with someone who was a bit more adventurous than other guys.

He bucked harder against my mouth and I had to grip the vibrator firmer to keep it from slipping out of my hand. Or from slipping out of him. I wanted to see him come with it inside his ass.

He let out a guttural, almost animalistic groan and his whole body went stiff except his hips. They moved faster and faster as he pounded himself deeper down my throat.

An even louder moan tore from his lips as he came, blasting hot, creamy cum into my mouth. Even after that, he kept on thrusting for a couple of minutes more.

Finally, his whole body flopped against the mattress and I slipped the vibrator out so he could get comfortable. I made a note to see what else he would let me use on him and how long he would keep them in there for.

"Holy shit," he whispered. "Just when I think you can't get any more amazing, you do. You blow my mind as well as my cock." He picked his head up and grinned. He really was too hot for his own good, and probably mine.

I laughed softly and dropped the vibrator onto the floor. "I try."

He pulled me up until my head rested against his chest and kissed my hair. "You do more than try. Everything you do, you kick ass. I can't imagine not having you in my life."

I tilted my head so I could look up at his face. "I can't imagine not having you in mine either." Or any of the guys, for that matter. Even Penn, as irritating as he was. If I was nice to him, maybe he would come around eventually. If not, that was his loss.

He was silent for a moment, then said, "I guess that journalist was right. We are sleeping together."

I snorted a laugh. "If that's news to you then I'm worried about your short term memory." There wasn't anything wrong with mine. I could vividly remember her accusing me of engineering publicity stunts to help my career. And then bringing up Zeke.

"How did she know anyway?" I asked. How did these people dig up all their dirt? I mean, the stuff they didn't make up.

"Lucky guess?" he suggested. "Or the fact you're living here."

I didn't miss the fact he referred to it that way and not that I was just staying here. This wasn't supposed to be a permanent arrangement, but I hadn't slept on the bed in the spare room even once. I didn't think he was planning to evict me anytime soon.

"How did she know I was living here?" I asked sleepily.

"That information could have come from any number of sources," he said. "It's not exactly a state secret."

"I guess not." I couldn't shake the uneasy feeling that crept up on me.

Amongst the people who knew were Reuben, Hunter and Parker. Hell, even Penn might have let it leak to cause trouble for me. Reuben might have thought it would embarrass me enough for me to scurry away and hide. If that's what he thought, then he would have to think again. I would stay here until either Zeke kicked me out or I decided to leave. I wouldn't be intimidated out the door. Not even by someone who probably had hitmen on speed dial.

Okay, maybe my ovaries were bigger than my common sense right now, but I wasn't going to run away again. I'd spent enough time over the last two years running from trouble and problems caused by other people. From now on, I was going to stand my ground as long as it remained more or less solid under my feet. I had several amazing guys who were very clearly ready to help me stay upright.

Figuratively speaking that was. At least three of them might have preferred me to be horizontal. At some point, I was going to have to figure that out. Was it even possible to go there with them and not jeopardise whatever this was growing between Zeke and I?

Saying the other guys in the band wanted to sleep

with me was one thing, but being okay with it actually happening was another.

Zeke muttered something I couldn't quite make out.

"What did you say?" I asked. I wasn't sure if he was trying to tell me something or if he was half asleep.

"I said I'm falling for you," he said.

17

ABBIE

"I SAID I'm falling for you."

His words echoed through my mind for days afterward. I hadn't answered. I couldn't come up with a coherent thought, much less the right response.

The next day, he acted like he hadn't said it all, so I didn't bring it up. I *wanted* to. A couple of times I almost did, but I chickened out at the last second.

Honestly, I wasn't sure what I'd say. I was falling for him too.

At the same time, I was developing feelings for the other guys in the band. Shit, what did that say about me? I struggled to have solid relationships with one guy at a time, much less a whole band of them. Surely they deserved better than someone who couldn't make up her mind?

These guys though, there was something about them all that made me want to tangle myself up tight, whatever the consequences. Around them I felt like maybe I could belong. To them and with them.

I needed that so badly. Ached for it. How could I walk away, especially when they seemed as invested in my career as they were in their own?

When the label wanted me to spend some time in the studio working on a new album, they came to give me support. Tully and Landon even offered to play on it.

So did Channing and Asher once the drummer was done complaining that he should have thought of it first.

However it came about, it was an offer I was ecstatic to accept.

I knew better than to hope Penn would offer, but I hoped he might. I've never heard anyone play keyboard like he did. He would make the album sound phenomenal.

Okay, *more* phenomenal.

Anyone the label chose would be amazing, but a girl could hope, right?

With that thought buzzing in my brain, I hurried

along the row of neat terrace houses about a block from Zeke's.

Each was about a hundred years old, but most were kept in good condition or recently renovated. One or two were for sale. I hated to think how much they'd be worth. With any luck, and a lot of hard work, I might get myself in a position where I could afford one some day. It was a nice area and convenient to everything.

Although, a small house in a leafy suburb would be nice too.

Or a harbourside mansion if I really wanted to stretch my imagination.

Even if I could afford somewhere like that, I wasn't sure if I wanted to live in a place that big. At least, not by myself. Maybe with the guys…

I was lost in that daydream when a dark car slid slowly past and pulled up by the side of the road, between a white hatchback and a red minivan.

Something about the tinted windows made my pulse spike and sweat break out under my arms.

I ducked my head and walked faster, resisting the sudden urge to run. I would have to pass it to get to Zeke's, unless I turned back and went the long way around.

Stop being fucking paranoid, I told myself. *There's a*

bajillion cars parked by the side of the road. This part of Sydney had almost no off-street parking. It wasn't even the only car with tinted windows.

In spite of giving myself that pep talk, the hair on the back of my neck rose when one of the back passenger doors opened.

It's nothing, I told myself. *Just a local doing their thang. Nothing to worry about.*

I was on edge after all the things that happened recently, and the fact I was alone for the first time in weeks.

The whole band was being interviewed on the other side of town, and the label needed me in the studio. Most of the guys weren't happy about it, but I reminded them I was a big girl and could take care of myself.

In the end, work was work.

I kept an eye on the car, but kept walking, albeit on the far side of the footpath, closest to the houses. Everything in me was on high alert. Fight or flight reflex at the ready. Should I turn and run?

No, I was fine. Everything was okay. I told myself that over and over.

Until I recognised the man who got out of the car.

"It's Abbie, isn't it?"

I wasn't sure if it was Hunter or Parker Brantley, but I doubted it was a coincidence he was here, on the same street I was walking up.

"Yeah. Hi." It didn't hurt to be polite, did it? Not yet at least. I stopped a couple of metres away from him.

I felt like a deer standing naked in front of a lion.

He smiled like we were old friends. "My brother wants to talk to you."

"Really?" I asked. "Which one? From what I've heard, you have a few."

His smile didn't falter. If anything, it got wider. "I can see why Zeke likes you. You've got balls. We both know you know I mean Reuben. And yet, you happily risk poking the hornet's nest."

I shrugged one shoulder. "You know what they say, you haven't lived until you've been bitten a few times."

He threw back his head and laughed. "I haven't heard that but I like it. I might make that my motto."

"You do that." I moved to step around him.

Just as quickly, he stepped back into my path. "I have to insist."

"He really does."

I didn't see the other twin leave the car, but

suddenly he was standing at my elbow. I almost jumped out of my skin.

I half turned and swallowed. I didn't want that to be a gun in his pocket, but I didn't want him to be happy to see me either. Guys like these didn't seem like they took no for an answer.

"Fucking hell," I muttered.

"Sorry, didn't mean to scare you." He didn't sound sorry at all. The opposite in fact.

I had a feeling these guys got off on scaring the shit out of people. No wonder Zeke didn't want anything to do with them.

"Sure," I said.

"Hunter, I don't think she believes you," the first guy said. Parker then.

"Fuck knows why." Hunter shrugged and waved towards the car. "In case you weren't sure, we're not asking."

"I didn't think you were," I said. "But I can give you my number if he wants to give me a call or send me a text."

Parker chuckled. "I'll take your number. But Reuben wants to see you in person." He slipped into the back seat and scooted across to the other side.

"Look how lucky you are, you get to sit between us," Hunter said. His eyebrow wiggle looked very much like Zeke's. No one could ever think they weren't related.

I swallowed. "Right. Lucky." I glanced around but no one seemed to be watching. No one was running down the street to stop them. "Is this going to take long?"

"It will take as long as it takes," Hunter said. He put a hand on my arm and pressed me towards the car. It wasn't quite a shove, but the message was clear. I could get in or he would force me in.

I thought about screaming, but if that was a gun in his hand, hidden by the fabric of his black hoodie, then things might end badly for me.

Of course, things could end badly for me if I got into the car. So I was either fucked, or I was fucked. Wonderful.

"If he wanted you dead, you would be dead," Hunter said.

I think he was trying to reassure me, but Reuben seemed like the kind of guy who could change his mind anytime he wanted to.

Since apparently I had no choice, I slid into the back of the car. Hunter climbed in next to me and closed the door.

I grabbed my seatbelt and clicked it into place. It

would be really fucking stupid to get into a crash and die, especially under the circumstances.

At some unseen signal, the driver pulled away from the curb and started to weave down the street and through Sydney traffic.

"Do you often do dirty work for your brother?" I asked conversationally.

"I have a feeling you want us to say this is a one-off," Parker said. "But it's not. We do shit like this for him all the time. What else are brothers for?"

I could think of a few things. "Is this what he wants Zeke back for? Why does he need him if he has you two?" And several other brothers to do his bidding.

"That's not for us to say," Hunter said. "But there are only two of us. We're pretty fucking epic, but we can't be everywhere." How modest he was.

"Have you tried?" I don't know why I was provoking these guys, but I couldn't seem to help myself. This, right here, might be why I got myself into trouble without meaning to.

It might also get me into a shallow grave.

"We've tried to be in the same place at the same time," Parker said. "It's a tight fit, but worth the effort. We'll be happy to show you after this if you like." He grinned.

It wasn't difficult to guess what he was referring to. "You're assuming there is an *after this*," I said.

Were they successful? No, wait, I didn't want to know. Mostly.

"That wasn't a no," he pointed out. "More and more I see why Zeke likes you. There's nothing better than an adventurous woman." He gave me a lopsided smile. No doubt he'd melted many panties in his day. He wasn't going to make me ruin mine.

"You mean one who puts out," Hunter said.

"That too," Parker agreed.

I rolled my eyes at neither of them in particular. If they weren't scary dudes, they might be hot. No, that's not true. They were definitely hot. Under very different circumstances, I might let them see if they could both fit their cocks into my pussy at the same time.

I absolutely did not sneak a speculative glance at Parker's groin. No way.

"I'm not sleeping with either of you," I said firmly.

"Who said anything about sleeping?" Parker actually gave me a wink. As if he and his brother hadn't abducted me off the street. He had a strange idea about seduction.

I snorted and turned my gaze towards the front windscreen of the car. I should probably have some idea where we were headed, in case I managed to get away from them and needed to know which direction to run.

Realistically, I wasn't likely to outrun two guys who were a foot taller than me and potentially armed. Especially not in heels.

"Is it far?" For all I knew, they were taking me to Melbourne or Dubbo, or who knew where else. Sydney was a big place.

There was a real possibility I could be dead in the next couple of hours. Or worse.

The humiliation of Poppy Newton's questions didn't seem quite so bad now.

For the umpteenth time in the last couple of years, I questioned my life choices. I could have taken a taxi back to Zeke's place, or stayed at the studio until the guys met me there.

Instead, I chose to walk by myself. A choice I made a million times before, in cities all over the world. Never with a killer on the loose, and Zeke's family lurking in the shadows.

I cursed myself, but I cursed the twins and Reuben even more. A woman should be able to walk around by herself wherever she wanted and not get hustled into the back of a car.

Or attacked. Or even wolf whistled at if she didn't want that to happen.

Fuck these guys.

Not literally.

"Not far," Hunter said lightly. "We've been staying close after what happened to Jonah. Reuben wants answers, as you can imagine."

"And he thinks I have them?" I asked. "I can tell you right now, I don't have a clue. Neither does Zeke." If we did, he probably would have told Reuben all about it, if only to keep him off our backs.

Parker shrugged. "You can tell him that. We're just doing what he asked."

"Do you ever tell him no?" They didn't seem like the kind of guys who rolled over and showed their tummy at the drop of a hat. They might be hounds, but not necessarily perfectly dutiful ones.

Both of them chuckled, but neither of them answered. That did absolutely nothing to alleviate my fear. On the contrary, I was more scared than ever.

18

ABBIE

WE PULLED up in front of a decent sized brick home, which looked like an old farmhouse. The area was farmland not that long ago, if I remembered right.

We were in the car for about an hour, and I didn't know this part of Sydney. If I had to run, I wouldn't have a clue which way to go, or where to find help.

Okay, fine, I would have to try charm instead. I might get out of this alive.

Or be totally fucked, because my mouth ran away when I was anxious, and right now I was scared as hell.

Please don't say anything to make them kill you, I begged myself. *Keep it together. Just long enough to get through this. Fall apart later.* That was good advice. Fingers crossed I would take it.

Parker opened the door beside him and climbed out of the car.

Hunter gestured for me to follow him.

"I like the back seat of a car as much as the next person, but you can get out now," Parker said teasingly.

I rolled my eyes towards the roof of the car and slid over so I could climb out. I did my best not to flash too much breast or leg in the process. I didn't think these two needed much encouragement and they certainly didn't need an eyeful.

"Thanks," I said sarcastically.

He grinned. "You're welcome. We can always spend a bit of time there after you speak to my brother."

"Do you ever give up?" I asked.

"Never," he replied easily. "You never know when a woman will change her mind. I can be persistent."

"No shit," I muttered.

"Me too." Just like out on the street, Hunter snuck up behind me and spoke suddenly.

They both chuckled when I jumped. Could anyone blame me for being startled? I was past being on edge and into whatever came after that. Somewhere just below full blown panic.

I glanced toward the street, but there was no

contingent of cop cars or anyone that looked like they were going to stop the twins from herding me into the house.

Rule number one of self defence was not letting yourself get taken to a secondary location. Having already failed that miserably, I had no choice but to walk between them to the front door of the house and inside.

"I don't know, but it doesn't seem like a good idea to leave the door unlocked to me," I remarked.

"Who said it was left unlocked?" Hunter asked.

We stepped inside and I saw a huge man with tattoos all the way up to his neck and across one side of his face. He wore a dark button down shirt and black jeans. He looked indifferently at all of us.

I presumed he was the one who unlocked the door. He must have been watching for us.

"Thanks, Terry," Parker said.

Terry grunted.

This huge, terrifying looking guy's name was Terry? For some reason, that made him seem a little less scary. Only a little. Mostly he was scary as fuck, like the twins.

"Boss is in the back." Terry jerked his head slightly toward a corridor.

Being an older home, it wasn't all open. The front

door led to a small foyer tiled with terracotta coloured tiles. Doors with dark architraves lined either side of the corridor. A staircase with the same dark stain and an ornate, square newel post, led up to the second floor.

Any other time, I would admire the history of the place. Today though, I barely paid any attention to it. I just wanted this to be over with. Whatever *this* was.

"This way." Parker started down the corridor and Hunter indicated that I should follow him. Having already scared the shit out of me twice, I didn't really want Hunter behind me, but it didn't seem like he was going to give me a choice.

Sticking with my decision to try to be nice, I walked quietly between the twins.

Parker led us all the way to the back of the house, to an enormous library.

Shelves stood from floor to ceiling and every centimetre was covered with books. None lay across the top of others, so I presumed they weren't book addicts, but they had enough of them that I almost reconsidered my assumption that Reuben was a homicidal asshole.

Almost. I mean, let's not go crazy here.

Reuben sat in the kind of leather armchair you might expect to see in an English library, or a movie.

If this was either of those things, he would look up from a leatherbound book and stare at me over a pair of glasses.

Instead, he was drinking a cup of coffee. At least, I presumed it was coffee, from the smell. If he wasn't completely evil, he would offer me a cup.

On the other hand, maybe it would be better not to take drinks from men like him.

He nodded at the twins and they both slipped out of the room.

I had no illusion that they would go far. Or that this man was harmless or even unarmed.

"Please, take a seat." He waved towards the armchair opposite him, as though he was doing nothing more than inviting me for a pleasant after-noon chat.

I kept half an eye on him, but moved over to perch on the edge of the chair.

"They said you wanted to talk to me." Why not get right down to it? I wasn't here for a good time.

Before he could respond, I said, "I don't know who killed Jonah. Neither does Zeke."

"I know," Reuben said simply. He took a sip of his coffee, then set it aside on the table beside his chair.

"Then why am I here?" He seemed to be a man of infuriatingly few words. If we kept up like this, I was going to be here three days before he got to the point.

"I want to talk about Zeke." He crossed his legs at his knees.

Okay, we were getting somewhere.

"What about him?" About a thousand thoughts tumbled through my head. Was this where he told me to stay away from his brother? That was up to Zeke, not Reuben. If he threatened to kill me in order to keep me away from his brother...

"I want you to convince him to leave the band," Reuben said.

I stared at him for a solid half minute.

Then I burst out laughing.

To the surprise of no one, he didn't laugh with me. He sat and looked back at me with one half raised eyebrow.

Yeah, probably a bad idea to laugh. I bit it down hard. "What makes you think he would listen to me even if I did ask him to do that? For one thing, he's under contract."

Reuben actually looked amused at that. "You of all people should know contracts can be broken."

Ouch. He knew exactly where to aim for a direct hit, didn't he? I was right, he was evil.

Or at least mean.

"In extreme circumstances they can," I agreed. "No offence, but I don't think, 'just because you say so,' would be considered extreme. No lawyer I ever met would argue that it is."

His half raised eyebrow became a three quarters raised eyebrow.

"Right, I've never met your lawyers." Of course he would have unscrupulous people on his payroll. Probably lots of them.

I tried another angle. "What about the fact he loves what he does? Doesn't that count for something?"

"He's been allowed to do what he loves for nearly a decade." He almost sounded reasonable. At least he believed what he was saying. I had to admire his conviction, even if it was horribly misguided.

"Why try to make him stop now? What's another decade or three between family?" That didn't seem like too much to ask to me. "Or better yet, let him go on living the life he loves."

I thought Reuben might get angry, and maybe he was, but he was controlled. He could have been carved from a block of ice.

"There are more important things in life than music," he said.

I snorted. "Says the man sitting in a room full of books."

There went that eyebrow again.

Since I already put my foot this far down my throat, I might as well keep going.

"How can you appreciate one art form and not another? It's not like you're sitting in a room full of classics or anything." I used that term in the traditional sense, not to insult any of the books in question. Which, at a quick glance around, were an eclectic selection, to put it mildly.

At least one shelf was taken up with romance novels. Either there was more to this man than met the eye, or this library wasn't just his. I couldn't remember if Zeke said anything about Reuben having someone in his life, nor had I asked. There was no accounting for taste.

"Reading books or listening to music are different to writing them, or making it," he said.

I squinted at him. "What would you read if authors stopped writing? If one of your other brothers came out as an author, would you want him to stop?"

"This isn't about speculation," he said.

"Then what is it about?" I thought for a little

while. "This isn't about Zeke doing what he loves, is it? You just want him to do what you tell him to do."

That was good news for any of his brothers if they were authors, but continued to be dutiful minions as well.

"I am head of the family," he said coldly. "I expect to be obeyed."

Yeah, and if this was a romance novel, I would be on my knees, calling him daddy.

Meanwhile, back in the real world, I wanted to punch him in the dick.

"I can talk to Zeke, but I'm not going to make any promises," I said. "I don't suppose you've considered a compromise? He works for you once in a while and stays with the band." I knew beyond a shadow of a doubt Zeke would never agree to something like that.

Reuben knew it too, I saw it in his intense, blue eyes.

"He won't compromise, and you won't," I concluded. "What if he never gives in and stays with the band forever?" I couldn't see him walking away. No time soon anyway, if ever.

"He will." Reuben nodded with absolute certainty. He leaned forward, elbows on the armrest of his chair, the fingers of one hand folded over the top of the other. "I can be persuasive."

"Yeah, I've heard that about the guys in your family," I said. "Did your parents never teach you no means no?"

He didn't answer that. He didn't need to.

I grimaced and said, "Is this where you tell me if I don't get through to Zeke, you're going to have me killed?"

"If necessary," he said coolly. He could have been talking about how blue the sky was today, or how the city could use more rain. Or less rain. Or something equally trivial.

Okay, I was hoping for a different response. One that resulted in me living a long, happy life. Preferably with Zeke and maybe the other guys.

I was thinking a little bit ahead here, but it wasn't every day someone told you they would kill you if they felt they needed to. I had no doubt he meant it. He wouldn't even blink if he picked up his phone right now and took out a hit on me. Or called Terry in to break my neck. He'd finish his coffee like nothing happened.

I should be more scared than I was, but if he needed my help, he'd need me alive for a while longer. In theory.

"Like I said, I'll talk to him. Honestly, though, I don't think I really have the kind of influence over him you think I do. We've only known each other for a couple of weeks." It felt like I had known him for years. Lifetimes.

"Then you're not as astute as I gave you credit for," Reuben said. "I saw the way he looked at you the other day. He obviously cares for you a great deal. Maybe even more than he realises. Certainly more than you realise."

Great, now I was getting relationship advice from the big bad wolf himself.

"And you care for him," he added. "You will want what's best for him."

"What if Wolf Venom is what's best for him?" I asked.

"It isn't. He just hasn't realised it yet."

19

ZEKE

"INTERVIEWS ARE my least fucking favourite part of this job," Asher declared.

"Yeah?" I squinted as we walked around the corner and I caught the dying rays of the sun right in my eyes. "You didn't look like you were hating it."

Of course not, he wasn't the one facing a barrage of questions about Abbie and her past. And my present, including my sex life. We usually didn't have a list of safe topics to discuss or ones which were off-limits, but I started to question that policy about halfway through.

Of course, fame brings with it an unhealthy interest in people's personal lives. That comes with the job. The last couple of relationships I had were with women who were also in the public eye. They knew the kind of questions I'd be asked and how much detail I was prepared to go into. I knew the same about them.

Abbie was different. Her past seemed to have generated some sort of unhealthy dislike from certain members of the media. Like that Poppy Newton woman, for one. The minute her name was linked with mine, I became a target of speculation too.

That didn't bother me. Their attitude toward Abbie did. And the idea that if they dug down deep, they would find out more about my family than I wanted anyone else to know.

"You know me, I go with the flow," Asher said lightly. "Also referred to as, 'no one gives a shit about the drummer.' I'm just the cute guy that sits in the back playing with his sticks."

"Very modest," I said ironically. He was right though, unfortunately. Tully and I came under the most scrutiny. Mostly me. That was what I got for being a hot and talented singer.

You had to take the good with the bad.

"Maybe we should rearrange the stage for the next tour," I said. "We can stick the drums out the front and the rest of us can hide behind you. We might start a new trend."

Asher chuckled. "That wouldn't work. Penny would want his pretty face out the front where people can see him."

He was one of the few people that got away with calling Penn 'Penny'. That didn't stop the rest of us from doing it once in a while, of course. Except Channing, who occasionally called him Beauregard. That always went down well. Not.

"You're not wrong." Penn did like to be noticed. Especially by the women in the crowd.

"Fine, we'll stick Penn out the front with you. I'll get a nice comfy armchair and sit in the back. Maybe a beanbag." I rubbed my hands together. That sounded comfortable, but not me at all. I liked to move around too much. And yeah, I liked to be seen too.

Asher laughed. "You can stay home and I'll make it a solo drum concert instead."

"Good luck with that," I said with a grin. Unfortunately for him, the drums were one instrument that couldn't really stand up by themselves, compared to others. If they could, no doubt he would be a smash hit. So to speak.

"Thanks. It could catch on. You could come along and sing on a few of my tunes." He gave me a playful shove with his shoulder as we walked.

"Isn't that what we're doing already?" I shoved him back. "You play and I sing along."

"When you put it that way, yeah. That's exactly what happens." He shoved me hard enough that I staggered sideways a few steps. "When our contracts are up, I should negotiate a bigger percentage."

I laughed and shoved him so hard his shoulder bounced off the front of the building beside us.

"Fuck, bro." He rubbed his shoulder, but he hadn't stopped smiling. "Careful with the money maker."

"You started it, bro," I pointed out.

"Yeah, well, I'm finishing it. Before one of us ends up on the road under a car." He waited a beat or two before shoving me again.

"Dickhead." I narrowly missed being pushed into the tree Abbie and I almost broke making out a couple of weeks ago. That much of my weight against it would have snapped it.

"You still love me," Asher said. "Who else would put up with your bullshit?"

"That list is longer than you think." I rubbed my arm. He was right though. He was more like a brother than any of my brothers. He was closer to me than he was to his brother or sisters as well. Although, he hadn't seen either of his sisters in a long time, so that wasn't much of a stretch.

"Okay, who would put up with your bullshit and keep smiling?" He paused and frowned. "What the fuck does that say about me? Maybe my standards should be a bit higher."

"Probably, but they're not," I teased. "Your standards are in the gutter, like mine."

He chuckled. "I think you just insulted the entire band, and Abbie."

"She's the exception," I said quickly. She was definitely way, way above the gutter.

I didn't know what the hell she saw in me, but I was glad she saw something. I meant what I said when I told her I was falling for her. Honestly, it might be an understatement. I was one hundred percent all right with that. I was happy to let myself fall head over heels in love with her. She was the most incredible, beautiful woman I ever met. We made beautiful music together, in and out of the rehearsal room.

"She really is," Asher agreed.

"Are you still thinking of asking her out?" I asked carefully.

"Thinking about it, planning it. Trying not to chicken out every time I get a moment to talk to her." He threw up his hands and let them drop to his sides.

"Asher DiMarco, if I didn't know better I would think you were shy." I shot a lopsided, teasing smile in his direction.

"Only around her," he admitted. "And this whole situation."

"If it wasn't for me, would you have asked her out already?" I asked.

"Yes. No. I don't know." He shrugged. "If it wasn't for you, there would still be the other guys in the band who look at her the same way I do. And then there's the whole thing about her being, you know, her."

"Yeah," I drawled. "You would be punching above your weight." I smiled slyly, then dodged out of the way when he swung at me.

"Fuck off," he said with a smile. "She and I would be a match made in heaven."

"Because she is an angel and you are a choirboy?" I asked. He was anything but. So was I, thank fuck. I hadn't been that sweet and innocent for a long time. Worst twelve years of my life.

"Because she is hot as fuck and I am hot as fuck," Asher said. "How could that be anything but perfect?"

"No idea, bro," I said. "Do you think it's possible

for a person to have more than one, I don't know, soulmate?"

"That is a deep question, bro," he said. "If you mean Abbie and I are both your soulmates, then I don't know how to answer that."

I snorted softly. "I meant her and me, and her and you, and her and any of the other guys. I know polyamory is a thing, but you think it's really possible to love several people equally?"

"I think…" he said slowly, "plenty of people seem to make it work. Parents love all of their kids equally, don't they?"

I gave him a look. "I don't know, do they?" My father had three favourites and none of them were me. He didn't mind telling us that either.

"Good point," Asher said. When his parents split, his mother took his sisters and his father took him and his brother. I remember him being absolutely convinced it was because they'd chosen their favourites. I always felt like it was as if they were dividing property, not preferring one or two children over the others.

"We love all of our songs equally, don't we?" he asked.

"I have three or four I like more than the others," I admitted.

"I guess sometimes it's hard not to have favourites," he said. "Like you love me more than any of the other guys in the band."

"That goes without saying." I looked over at him for a few beats and smiled.

He smiled back. "Love you too, bro. I know you've always got my back."

"And you've always got mine." We understood each other's crazy lives and families better than anyone else. It was just one of those cases of if you know, you know. We definitely knew. We told the other guys almost everything, but living it was a different story.

"Even when you're being a dickhead," he said lightly.

I snorted a laugh. "Luckily that only happens on rare occasions."

"But you admit to being a dickhead once in a while?" he asked.

"I even admit to being a fuckwit from time to time," I said. "Just don't tell anyone I said so."

"Your secret's safe with me." He nodded.

I stopped as we drew closer to my front door. The city was bathed in golden twilight and mid-spring warmth, but a chill travelled down my spine.

"What is it?" Asher stopped too.

I knew he trusted my instincts. If I felt like something was off, then something was off.

I shook my head and turned around slowly, eyes and ears open. "I don't know." Nothing looked like it was out of place. At least, nothing I could put my finger on.

"Let's get inside. I want to make sure Abbie is okay." It was times like this I wished I carried a gun. A Glock in my hand right now might make me feel a tad better.

I pulled out the key from my pocket and hurried up to my door.

No cardboard box. No broken lock. No sign of forced entry. No sign of anything.

And yet, the hairs on the back of my neck stuck up and tingled.

I pushed the door in and looked around before I stepped inside. Still, nothing looked out of place. The townhouse was silent and dark.

"Abbie?" I called out softly.

No reply.

"She might be asleep," Asher suggested. "Otherwise, I think she would have put some lights on."

"Right." That was a good point. "Stay down here. I'm going to check upstairs."

I walked up the timber steps as silently as I could.

If she was asleep, I didn't want to wake her. If she wasn't asleep and someone else was here, they would have heard us enter the building anyway.

I slipped upstairs and peeked into the spare room. It was empty and the bed was still as neatly made as the day she moved in. We hadn't talked about it, but she spent every night in my bed.

I glanced into the open door of the bathroom. That was empty too.

The last room was my bedroom and ensuite. If she was up here, she'd be in there.

I pushed open the half closed door and winced as it creaked. I should get that oiled. On the other hand, it made a good alarm if anyone tried to sneak up on me in the middle of the night.

I peered inside. There was enough light coming in the window to see around the room.

"Fuck." It too was empty.

"Where are you?" I pulled my phone out of my back pocket and glanced at it. There was no message from her on the screen. No missed calls. Nothing.

My heart started to race. If Reuben did something to her...

I trotted back down the stairs. "She's not up there."

"Shit," Asher said softly. "Do you think…"

"If he has, I'm going to rip his fucking face off," I growled.

A car engine thrummed closer until it pulled up outside. We exchanged glances.

It got harder to breathe.

20

ZEKE

Sweat sprang up on my hands and under my arms.

Like a shadow, I slipped into the kitchen, crouched and silently, gingerly, opened the bottom drawer of the cabinet. I felt around for a moment before I pulled out a fully loaded Glock.

Asher dropped down beside the couch to pull out the other one. Only he and I knew where I kept my firearms. As far as the rest of the band knew, I didn't own one.

That was technically correct. I *didn't* own one, I owned *three*.

The other was upstairs in my bedroom. If anyone tried to creep up on me in my own home, they weren't getting away unscathed.

The car door opened, followed by the sound of muffled male voices.

And a female voice.

Asher and I exchanged glances.

He mouthed, "Abbie?"

I frowned and listened carefully. It sounded like her, but I couldn't tell if she was distressed or not.

If they hurt a hair on her head, I was going to blow their nuts off.

I crept toward the door.

It was still half closed from when we entered the townhouse.

I raised my foot and carefully nudged it the rest of the way open. Unlike my bedroom door, the front door didn't squeak. It moved silently on well oiled hinges.

Footsteps hurried towards the front door, but whoever it was, was obscured by the bushes out the front.

I raised my gun.

Abbie came around the corner and froze. Her eyes widened at the sight of the barrel pointed right at her face. She let out a squeak and her lips dropped apart. She raised her hands to either side and stared.

"Jesus fucking Christ." I lowered the gun. "Are you all right?"

She looked shaken, pale.

"Um. I could use a drink." Even her voice was shaking.

I put a hand on her upper arm and gently pushed around behind me. "Who's in the car?"

I took a step towards the street just as the vehicle peeled away from the curb. The tinted windows meant I couldn't see inside, but I could guess.

Motherfuckers.

"Go inside. Asher is in there. I'll make sure they've gone." I gripped my Glock tighter and gave her a reassuring nod.

"Zeke…be careful," she whispered.

"Always," I said over my shoulder. "Don't worry, I'll be fine." My relatives, on the other hand—

I stepped past the bushes and looked down the street. It was empty except for the usual cars parked along either side. The dark car that dropped her off was gone.

Lucky for them.

The street lights flickered on as if to punctuate that the assholes who took Abbie were gone now.

I hurried back inside the house, closed and locked the door behind me.

Abbie and Asher stood in the kitchen, his arm

around her shoulders, a drink of what looked like bourbon in her hands.

In full view of them both, I put the Glock back in the drawer and closed it. I didn't care if Abbie also knew where it was. She might need to know someday.

I poured myself and Asher a glass of bourbon each and passed his to him. We didn't usually drink it straight, but this seemed a good time to make an exception.

"What happened?" Asher asked.

Abbie's face was still pale, but the colour slowly started to return. She took a sip of bourbon and grimaced at the taste.

"Reuben wanted a little chat," she said.

"Fucker," I spat. "What about?" I had a few suspicions.

"He wanted me to convince you to leave Wolf Venom." She half shrugged. "I told him I didn't think you would listen to me."

"On that subject, I won't listen to anyone," I growled. "He should know that by now."

He *did* know that, he just didn't know when to give up and admit defeat. Would he ever learn? I fucking hoped so. I was past done with him and his blind persistence.

"That's basically what I said." She licked bourbon from her lower lip. "He seems to think leaving the band would be the best thing for you."

I laughed bitterly. "He wouldn't have a clue what is best for me." Only, he knew well enough to take her and not one of the guys.

"Did he touch you?" I would hunt his ass down and feed it to him if he did.

"No," she said quickly. "He was almost...amicable."

"That sounds like Reuben," Asher said. "He likes to pretend he's reasonable. I'm pretty sure most of the time he's plotting to have someone pull out my pubic hairs one by one, then take my kneecaps and feed them to his pet cockatiel."

I snorted because that was specific and somewhat accurate. Except for the part about the cockatiel. Reuben wasn't much of an animal lover.

"Honestly, I was half expecting him to give me to the twins to do whatever they wanted." Her voice shook again. "Would they actually do that?"

The fear in her voice ignited my anger again.

"Parker and Hunter like to pretend they're nice guys, like Reuben," I said slowly. "But they'll just as quickly shoot you or gut you if he told them to. I wouldn't put anything past either of them."

To my knowledge, neither of my brothers ever raped a woman, but that didn't necessarily mean they hadn't. I didn't keep tabs on them twenty-four hours a day, seven days a week.

Or at all.

Maybe I should start doing that. I could afford to have a private investigator follow them around. Although, they would probably kill them and hide the body in a shallow grave, so that would be a waste of money.

And, you know, the life of the investigator.

"I'm so sorry." I took a big gulp of bourbon. I might need a lot more of it to get through the next couple of hours. "You shouldn't have been dragged into any of this."

It was Asher who responded. "It's not your fault, Zeke. You can't help who your family is any more than I can. It's their fault this happened. It's Reuben's fault he won't let you live your life. He should fuck off and leave you alone."

I sighed. She was right, but it didn't make any of this any better.

"Maybe I should leave the band when my contract is up, before someone gets killed for me." Was it stupid or selfish to put people at risk just so I could sing and entertain people?

No one deserved to die so I could keep doing that. I might take up a hobby instead. I could learn to knit. How hard could that be?

"No," they both said in unison.

"The band is your life," Abbie said.

"Unless you're sick of us." A slight smile tugged at the corners of Asher's mouth. "I can be annoying sometimes."

"You cannot," Abbie said. "At least, not as far as I've seen."

He smiled a little more and lightly kissed her mouth. "That's sweet of you to say."

Damn, why was that hot? There wasn't even a hint of jealousy there, I wanted to watch them kiss a bit more.

When we all calmed down.

"You're not that annoying," I told him. "No more than I am, and I prefer you all alive. Is making music really worth the hassle and the risk?" The idea of losing either of them made my heart squeeze almost to the point of pain. They were both my people.

"An unreserved yes," Abbie said. "Would I put up with all the gossip and humiliation if it wasn't?"

"Neither of those end in you being dead," I pointed out.

"They might as well," she said softly. "You have no

idea how brutal it's been. I think I'd rather face your brothers than people like Poppy Newton."

I supposed it was all a matter of perspective, because I would much rather deal with the press. Although, I hadn't had my name dragged through the mud.

Yet.

There was still plenty of time for that to happen. Honestly, I'd be the first to admit the media treated men better than women. Chances were, I'd get off lightly compared with what Abbie went through.

"We should put that in the 'let's talk about it later' pile and order some dinner," I said. "If any of us can eat."

Otherwise, we could just get drunk instead. Who knows what might happen then?

"I could eat," Asher said. Judging by the way he glanced at Abbie, he wasn't just talking about food.

"I'm hungry too." She looked at him the same way.

Holy hell, my heart raced faster than it had when I heard the car pull up out the front.

I swallowed. "I'll grab the takeaway menus."

"Yeah," Asher agreed. "Maybe something hot."

Call me old-fashioned, but I had a bunch of paper menus in a pile in the corner of the kitchen. I would order with my phone, not because I wasn't a complete Neanderthal, but I prefer to look over the menu and scratch off anything I tried and didn't like. I didn't scratch off much.

I picked up the pile and hunted through them. "Indian? Thai?"

"There goes that myth," Abbie said. When I looked at her questioningly, she added, "I thought guys only ordered pizza when they ordered in."

"We're enlightened gentlemen," Asher said proudly, laughter in his voice.

"Yes, we are," I agreed.

I couldn't get past the vibe in the room. It was as though the adrenaline of what happened to Abbie had translated to sexual tension.

What did that say about us that we got off on bad things happening? I suppose we were all as fucked up in the head as each other.

So were the rest of the guys in the band, now I thought about it. They'd probably find this evening's events exciting. Thank goodness no one died.

Yet.

"I'll eat whatever." Asher took his eyes off Abbie long enough to give me a shrug.

"Me too." I handed Abbie the menus so she could decide. As long as she was happy, I didn't give a shit what I ate. As long as I was near her. And Asher too.

My heightened awareness of them both was probably reading things into this that weren't there.

On the other hand, I was usually very keyed in to situations like this. I met countless groupies and learned how to discern whether they were interested or just flirting. If they wanted one night or something more.

This was definitely something more and it wasn't just me and Abbie or Abbie and Asher.

What was it then? What I felt for Asher was closer than brothers but was there something else to it? Something I hadn't realised until now?

Or, I realised it but hadn't acknowledged it? I always thought he was adorable, but more than that never even crossed my mind. Had it crossed his? Should I push these thoughts back into a box and shut the lid before I did something I'd regret?

The last thing I wanted to do was fuck up our friendship. For one thing, the guy knew where I kept my guns.

Abbie's tongue darted over her lips and she looked over the menus.

"What about a Madras chicken and lamb tikka? And some rice. And beer."

"Lots of beer." I grabbed up my phone and placed the order. "It shouldn't be long."

I took the menus from Abbie's hands, put them aside and drew her closer to me.

I pressed my mouth lightly to hers. She tasted of salt and bourbon. I deepened the kiss, letting my tongue taste hers, then drew back.

Asher put a hand on her cheek, turned her face to him and kissed her. His tongue pried her lips open and explored the inside of her mouth.

She let out a soft moan which made my cock hard as a rock.

Asher broke off the kiss and drew back from her.

I thought he'd pull back to let me take another turn.

Instead, he kept one hand on her cheek and leaned over to kiss my mouth.

It was unexpected, but it sent a wash of fire through my entire body.

"Holy shit," Abbie whispered. "That's so hot."

I couldn't disagree, especially since my mouth was busy kissing him back, my tongue tracing his lips. He tasted as good as she did.

When he broke off from me, I kissed her again. My erection was almost painful. If we kept doing this, I was going to come right here in the kitchen.

"We should probably... Dinner won't be long..." Apparently Asher was having as much trouble with coherent thought as I was right now.

I glanced down at his groin. Not surprisingly, he looked as hard as I felt. What would it be like to touch him? Or watch him fuck Abbie? God, I wanted both of those things. And to fuck her myself. Was that greedy?

I decided it wasn't. What was the point of life if you couldn't live it? And enjoy as much of it as possible.

21

ABBIE

I ADJUSTED my headset and got ready to sing again.

Having been in the studio for four hours, I was ready for a break. At the same time, I wanted to get this song down right.

I wrote "Nothing Under My Feet" when I was at my lowest point. I was waiting for the annulment from Vance and the press was blowing up my phone and knocking on my door for interviews. I couldn't leave my apartment without being followed, stared at and photographed. They didn't want nice photos either. They wanted candid ones of me dressed in track pants with my hair in disarray. Or better yet, in a compromising position with somebody else.

At the time, I was barely able to get out of bed, much less go out and do anything embarrassing. The stupid thing was, I never much cared if anyone caught me in a compromising position, but the press made it all so ugly and sordid.

Vance added fuel to the fire every chance he got. Asshole.

Maybe I should have made a deal with Reuben; I would speak to Zeke if he had Vance dealt with.

Okay, I wouldn't really ask anyone to do that. Probably.

That begged the question—would Reuben make a deal like that? I had a feeling he would do whatever it took to get his brother to return to the flock. Just like Zeke would do whatever it took to avoid it.

It was not a good situation to be in the middle of.

Asher and Zeke were a much better place to be in the centre of. Watching them kiss the other night still sent sparks of heat all through me.

I wanted to be with both of them and it was pretty clear the feeling was mutual all around. As soon as we finished dinner, Landon and Channing turned up at the door. We ended up having a movie marathon and falling asleep curled up on the couch together. All five of us. I could very easily get used to doing things like that.

"Okay, from the top again," Candy, the producer, said from inside her booth.

I nodded. It was just me in here right now. Later, the instruments would be recorded and then the whole thing would be mixed. I would have liked to record with the instruments in here with me, but it was easier to concentrate when I only had to worry about my vocals.

I took a quick gulp of water and started to sing into the microphone on the stand in front of me.

"The ground is broken,
the air is shattered,
my world is nothing but an echo.
You stole my heart and ripped it out.
Now there's nothing under my feet.

I'M FALLING HARD,
you're not there to catch me.
You watched me tumble to my knees,
you broke me down,
you tore my last breath.

NOW THERE'S NOTHING UNDER my feet.
Nothing to stop me.
Nowhere to hide.
Nothing under my feet.

. . .

I LANDED HARD,

but I got up.

I won't let you take my everything away.

I'll walk away from you,

stronger than before.

I have everything under my feet."

I LIFTED my chin as I sang the last note.

Somewhere in the middle of writing that song, I realised I couldn't let Vance win. Or the press, for that matter. I had to get back up on my own two feet and live my life the way I wanted to. That included releasing this song. It was a long time coming, but it was the public 'fuck you' he deserved.

No one would doubt who was aimed at.

Maybe I shouldn't give him another fifteen minutes of fame, but I needed to get it off my chest. I wanted everyone to know I intended to live my best life from here on out. And if they didn't like it, that was their problem.

"Great work." Candy Davis was one of the best in the business.

Of course, White Wolf Records wouldn't

compromise. Levi Jones hadn't built a successful label by cutting corners. He did it by hiring and signing the best and putting them together in the studio.

"Let's take a break." Candy took off her headphones and set them aside before she stepped out of the booth. "It must feel good to get back on the horse. So to speak."

I slipped off my headphones and smiled. "God, yeah, it really does. I didn't realise how much I missed this."

"If you don't mind me saying, you sound even better than anything I heard on the radio," she said. "The time away has given your voice an emotion and richness you either didn't have before, or your previous producer didn't manage to bring out."

"I guess there is an upside to life fucking you over," I said ironically. I knew what she meant though. Nothing I did before was as personal as the stuff I was working on for the new album. I felt it all in a way I hadn't on the last two. Like everything was coming from the heart now, not just my vocal cords.

"You're easy to work with too," Candy added. "I can't say that about a lot of people." She gave me a, 'what are you going to do,' look.

"Let me guess, you thought I would be a nightmare because of my reputation?" I tucked a strand of hair behind my ear.

She wouldn't be the first or the last to make that assumption. I tried to be respectful of the people I worked with, because a good producer could help elevate my career higher than I dared to dream.

"Something like that," she agreed unapologetically. "I don't pay a whole lot of attention to gossip or tabloids or any of that shit, but people talk, whether we like it or not. I usually don't believe half of it until I've actually worked with them. Some people are way worse than rumours suggest."

I had a list of them off the top of my head, starting with Vance and ending with Penn.

"How do you go working with Penn?" I couldn't resist asking.

"He's a pain in the ass," Candy said. "He's still not the worst of them, though. I've had a couple who refused to work with a woman. You can imagine how that went down with the bosses."

"Not very well," I guessed. "Did they replace you?"

She grimaced as we stepped through the doors into the small lunchroom. "In one case they did, or the artist would have walked. They put their foot down the other time. Giving in to stupid demands isn't a good habit to get into."

"Amen to that." I picked up a sandwich in a plastic container and filled up a cup with coffee before taking them over to a table.

It wasn't much, but I was grateful the label supplied lunch at all. Staying with Zeke saved me a lot of money, but I was starting to run out of it. Everywhere I could cut costs, I had to. That included eating prepackaged lunches and bad instant coffee. It was better than going hungry.

Candy slid into the chair next to me, her bright pink ponytail swinging. "I can't imagine working anywhere else, even if there are jerks around. Even if those jerks can't keep their hands to themselves sometimes."

"I can relate to that," I said wryly. "Some see a woman in the industry and think she's fair game."

"Especially if we're wearing a skirt." She bit into her sandwich like she was taking her frustrations out on the bread.

"Right?" I couldn't remember the last time I sat down for a friendly chat with another woman. It was nice. "I used to work with a producer who would try to stick his hand up my skirt every chance he got. I was new in the industry and he was a lot older than me. He seemed to think there was nothing wrong with it."

Candy's eyes widened. "I wish I could say I hadn't heard the same thing a thousand times before, but I have. What did you do?"

"What could I do?" I asked. "He was powerful and I was a total no one. I had no choice." I paused for a moment before I added, "I started wearing pants. I don't think he ever figured out how to handle it."

Candy laughed. "That's perfect. Of course, we shouldn't have to change our wardrobes just because of people like that."

I sipped my coffee and sighed. "No, we shouldn't. I would never refuse to work with a producer, but I like working with a woman. It's a pleasant change."

"I guarantee I will never stick my hand up your skirt," Candy said.

"That's good to know." I had a funny feeling, if anyone tried anything inappropriate with me, the guys in the band would have something to say about it. They had enough influence to get a producer fired if they wanted to. Or killed.

She tilted her head and her ponytail dropped out to the side. "You aren't what I expected at all."

"You expected a self-centred, arrogant bitch?" I suggested. "The kind of person who is only interested in fame and fortune. Who would get married just to cause a stir?"

I didn't speak with more than a hint of bitterness. I was used to people expecting that of me by now, and being surprised when it wasn't what they got.

"I don't know what I expected," she admitted. "A lot of the artists have their heads up their bums. Or they looked terrified to be here if this is their first time in the studio. You don't. You seem like you're at home here."

That was such a sweet thing for her to say, I thought I might cry.

"Everyone at the label has been amazing. When Jackson said it was one big happy family, I thought he was full of shit." Especially with Penn giving me death glares every five minutes. "But it kinda seems like everyone makes the effort to look out for each other."

The band certainly welcomed me with open arms, for the most part.

"Levi Jones figured out the best way to make a shit load of money was to keep everyone happy," Candy said. "We try to make as few waves as possible, as much as possible. The label motto should be' we make music, not waves'." She grinned.

I laughed. "That sounds about right. I wish I signed on with White Wolf to start with. That would have saved me a lot of heartache."

"Yeah, but would you sing as well if you hadn't been through all that?" she asked.

I wasn't sure how to answer that. "I don't know," I said slowly. "I'd like to think so. If not, then I guess all the drama was worth it in the end. At least something good came out of it."

"That's a good way to look at it," she said. "We can't change the past, but we can appreciate the person it moulded us into."

"That's very poetic," I said. "Are you a songwriter as well as a producer?"

"Yeah. And I sing and play a few instruments. I guess you could call me an all-rounder. There's no aspect of the music industry I don't adore. Except maybe the cheap coffee."

She sipped hers and made a face. "You know what, you should come out with me and the girls sometime. We could go out to a club, dance and all that shit."

"I'd like that," I said. I hadn't had much in the way of female friends for a while. Not that I kept in touch with anyway. As much as I loved hanging out with the guys, it would be nice to have some female company once in a while.

22

ZEKE

"THANKS FOR COMING WITH ME," I said.

Asher glanced over at me from behind the steering wheel. "I could totally take that the wrong way, but I'm not going to."

I snorted. "Sure you're not." Things could have gotten awkward between us, but thank fuck they hadn't. If anything, it felt more comfortable. Like somehow we resolved something we hadn't known was unresolved.

In truth, we hadn't really resolved anything, apart from admitting we had a mutual attraction to each other as well as Abbie.

Since I was a kid, I've known I was bi, but I never gave it much thought, much less exploration. It was just another aspect of myself, like my eye colour. I never considered finding a guy to experiment with.

Until now, it was just about looking and appreciating attractive people, regardless of their sex.

"Okay, I am," he admitted. "Do you want to talk about the other night?"

"I don't know, do you?" I put my elbow on the armrest, placed my head on my hand and looked over at him.

I always considered him an attractive guy, but that had a whole new slant now. I saw him the same way I saw Abbie. At the same time though, he was my oldest, best friend. I didn't want to screw this up. I would never forgive myself if I ruined everything between us. If nothing else, he knew exactly what having a family like ours felt. We confided in each other in ways I didn't with the other guys. Shared war stories, as it were. Or survival stories.

"I think we should," he said. "If only to make one thing clear."

Okay, here it came. This was where he told me it was the bourbon talking. That he regretted kissing me. That he felt weird around me now.

I hurt myself thinking like that. My heart squeezed in my chest.

"What's that?" I asked carefully. It might be a wise

move to listen to what he had to say before I jumped to conclusions. Yeah, as if the human brain is that rational.

He cleared his throat. "What I did, kissing you. I didn't just do that so I could kiss Abbie too. Or because of the adrenaline, or the alcohol. I did it because I wanted to kiss both of you. I'm sorry if this makes it weird, but I've been wanting to do that for a long time. It seemed like the right time, the other night."

I let out a hard exhale of relief.

"It doesn't make it weird," I said fiercely. I was beyond relieved that he had no regrets. "I'm glad you did it. I liked it, and I know she did too." She looked like she flooded her panties watching us. Remembering the expression on her face made my balls ache and cock twitch.

He grinned. "That's awesome," he said, tone as relieved as mine. "And about me kissing Abbie. You didn't mind?"

"Nope," I replied lightly. "It was kinda hot to watch."

"Yeah? It was kinda hot to watch you two, too. Now I get why Landon and Channing are into sharing the way they are. I should have known these guys were onto something long ago.

They must be smarter than they look." He chuckled.

"That wouldn't be too hard," I joked. Both of the guys were very smart, like all of us, but I couldn't resist making a light dig at them.

Asher laughed. "Fuck, I'm glad this didn't get strange. I was worried you would punch me in the face or something."

"Really?" I frowned at him. "I seem like the kind of guy who would do that?" Ouch.

"No, but you never know what people might do in the heat of the moment," he said. "Especially after what happened with Abbie."

"I guess so." I shrugged. "Lucky I didn't still have a gun in my hand."

"Luckyily neither did I," he retorted. "That could have ended badly for everyone."

"Right." That was one reason I wasn't the biggest fan of guns. They tended to hurt people sometimes. Strange how that went.

"So, have you ever—" Asher paused with his mouth open, searching for the right words.

I had a pretty good idea of what he was trying to ask, but I couldn't resist stirring him up a little.

"Have I ever what?" I asked with mock innocence.

"Um. Been with another guy?" he said in a rush.

"Ahhh," I said slowly. "No, I haven't. Have you?" I went from picturing him with Abbie, to picturing him with Abbie and another guy.

Was it this hot in the car when I got inside it?

"Yeah, a couple. No one you know, just people I met on tour." He stopped the car at a red traffic light.

My eyebrows twitched. You think you know a guy, and then you realise you don't know as much as you thought you knew. I was glad he felt comfortable telling me all of this though. We were usually frank about our sex lives when it came to women, and Landon and Channing talked about their time with each other as well as women, but this was new for Asher and I.

After a few moments of hesitation, I asked, "What's it like?"

It was his turn to pause. "It's like...sex. The mechanics are a little different, but the feelings are the same."

I nodded slowly. "Gotcha. That's good to know." It was. Admitting to an attraction and acting on it were two different things. Rushing in could be bad for everyone.

"Do you think you could ever..." He glanced over at me, then back at the road as the light turned green.

"I don't know," I admitted. "I think so. This is all kinda new to me."

"Of course," he said quickly. "I didn't mean to pressure you."

"You didn't," I assured him. "You know me, I can say no when I need to."

"You definitely can," he agreed. "You've been saying no to your brother all this time and you've stuck to it."

I wasn't sure how much longer that would last, but I didn't tell him that. He already knew I was considering going back. I knew there was no chance Abbie and the other guys would let me go without a fight.

At the end of the day, this had to be my choice, just like it would be my choice to fuck Asher or any other guy.

"Yeah," I said lightly. "And Reuben is scarier than you."

"You wound me," Asher said jokingly. "I'm really scary, like all us DiMarcos."

"Okay, you're right. You're the second scariest DiMarco I know. Second only to Dane."

"Fair call," Asher said. "Dane is a scary guy. One of the top three scariest, after Reuben and your other brother, Caleb."

"It's difficult to separate the three of them," I remarked. Was it bad that I liked the fact Caleb lived in Melbourne and I hardly saw him? He was as much fun to hang out with as Reuben. Joshua wasn't much better. Or the twins for that matter. Lucas was mostly harmless, ish. Funny that I ended up the nice guy of the family.

"Sometimes I wonder why we joined a rock band and didn't go into witness protection," Asher said, half jokingly.

"Because we have talent we have to share with the world," I said modestly.

"Oh yeah, that sounds about right." He nodded. "I knew there had to be a good reason. I mean, we put up with a lot of crap from them, don't we?"

"Too much," I agreed. That was what today was about. While Abbie was in the studio recording her new album, which I knew was going to be incredible, Asher and I would deal with some things. She was safe enough there and Candy knew to watch out for her.

If there was anyone outside the band I trusted with Abby's safety, it was Candy. She was a small woman, but her tiny size and bright pink hair caused many people to underestimate her. In reality, she had mad skills in more martial arts than I knew actually existed. Abbie was as safe with her as she was with me.

"How long do you think it will be before Penny realises he's as hot for her as the rest of us?" Asher asked.

"Penn is hot for us all?" I grinned.

Asher snorted. "Probably, we're us. But that wasn't what I meant."

"No shit," I teased. "I don't know. Penn is even more stubborn than I am. He'll at least spend another couple of weeks grumbling about her being around, and giving her dirty looks. And telling everyone how much he wants her to go away."

"Meanwhile, he probably has a photo of her on his phone he can masturbate to." Asher grinned.

"Are you projecting?" I asked.

Great, now I had a mental image of Asher with his phone in one hand and the other curled around his hard cock. Only in this scenario, it wasn't a photo of Abbie, it was a video call and she was naked with her hand between her legs.

It was definitely getting hotter inside the car. I wound the window down a little bit.

"I might be," Asher agreed. "I only have your word on how amazing she is."

I smiled slowly. "You do, don't you? Sucks to be you."

He groaned. "You had to mention sucking."

I groaned playfully in response. "You had to interpret my words as a blowjob."

I wasn't thinking that at all. Well, now I was.

"Yes. Yes I did," he said. "You know, some people like to go down on a guy while he's driving."

Now there was a suggestion that would make a guy hot under the collar. Or a woman too, no doubt. How would it feel to wrap my lips around his cock? The idea made my balls hurt.

I looked over. "My head wouldn't fit between your cock and the steering wheel." Also, that might come under the banner of rushing.

"I can pull over," he said.

I glanced out the window. "No you can't. Not on a road like this. Maybe you could concentrate on driving before you get us both killed."

"That might be the most sensible thing you've said all day." He exhaled loudly out his nose. "Not even a blowjob is worth getting killed for."

"Are you sure about that?" I asked. "Maybe you haven't had a good enough blowjob."

"Possibly not," he said slowly. "Are you saying you've had a blowjob worth dying for?"

"Well, I don't want to brag." I grinned. "I did tell you Abbie is amazing."

"Shit, dude, I want to be you when I grow up. Actually, no I don't. I'd be happy to be *with* you when I grow up. When you're ready, that is. If you're ready," he added quickly.

"When I'm ready, you'll be the first to know," I assured him. Of course he would. Being with another guy would feel like cheating on Asher, just like being with another woman would feel like cheating on Abbie.

When the hell had things gotten so complicated? I think it started with that night in the dark corner of the club, when a beautiful blond woman let me slip my hand up her skirt and into her pussy.

Or maybe it started a million years ago when the dust that would become us started to form. I wasn't a big believer in fate until now. What else could it be?

We all made beautiful music together, in perfect pitch.

What I wasn't sure of was where the other guys fit into this. All I knew was that I was certain they did. We were like a jigsaw puzzle with seven pieces. Abbie was the very centre piece. I was the piece that slotted in right beside her. Penn was the piece that was shaped unusually, so it didn't seem to fit at all until you found just the right spot for it. Everyone else had their own place. We just had to figure out exactly where they went to finish off the puzzle.

If only my brother and people like him didn't sweep us off the table and scatter the pieces before that could happen.

"I hope so," Asher said so softly I almost missed hearing him speak.

23

ZEKE

"DUDE, your brother has eclectic taste in books." Asher pulled one out from the shelf and looked at the bare-chested football player on the cover.

"I'm sure Lizzi Stone is amazing, but she doesn't seem like your brother's taste." He put the book back and pulled out another.

"Aaron L. Speer," he read. "At least this one is mafia."

I snorted at the irony.

Asher opened the book in the middle and started to read.

His eyes widened. "I was already horny enough. If I keep reading this, I'm going to blow my head off." He closed the book and put it back on the shelf.

"I didn't realise you were so flexible," I teased.

"You have no idea." He grinned.

I wasn't sure if the mental image of Asher sucking his own cock was arousing or disturbing. I might think about that more later, when I wasn't as anxious as I was right now.

Terry had let us into the house and told us to wait in the library.

That was at least half an hour ago. Either Reuben was too busy to see us straight away, or he was pretending he was.

It was very much like him to let us sweat, just to toy with us. Of course, if I tried to call him out on it, he would point out we turned up unannounced. Whatever I said, he would make it my fault, so I wouldn't say anything.

I'd wait patiently until he was good and fucking ready to see us.

"Lily Luchesi, I've heard of her." Asher pulled out another book from the shelf and took it over to sit in a chair and read. He seemed a lot less anxious than I felt. "She writes about vampires, but it's still not your brother's style."

I shrugged and leaned my shoulder against the wall. "They might be Parker's books. Or Terry's."

Asher laughed.

I stifled a chuckle at the idea of the big guy reading romance books. Or any book, for that matter.

Personally, I preferred to read thrillers, and cozy mysteries, but I've read a few romances in my day, when there was nothing else to read. Okay, and because I liked them, but that was a closely guarded secret I'd never admit to.

"Your brother isn't seeing anyone, is he?" Asher asked. "He doesn't secretly have a woman stashed away around here?"

"Why, are you interested in him?" I asked jokingly.

"Hell no." Asher glanced up from his book and made a face. "It would explain these books, that's all."

"Maybe Reuben is getting soft in his old age," I said. "He might want to read about love because the only way he would find it is if he paid for it or bribed her."

The first sign I had that Reuben stepped into the library was the sound of him clearing his throat. Of course he arrived just in time to hear me say that. Figured. Whatever, I was going to piss him off one way or another.

I turned around unapologetically and resisted the strong, initial urge to punch him in the face.

He looked at me like something nasty he found on the bottom of his shoe. Something he wouldn't even bother to scrape off. He would just throw the shoe away, or burn it.

"Ezequiel, have you come to tell me you've quit your little band?" he asked.

I hated when he called me that and he knew it. It was so unfair that he didn't have a longer version of his name. He had a shorter version though, one he hated with fierce loathing.

"Ruby, no, I haven't." I gave him a smug smile and crossed my arms over my chest.

Round one was a tie.

Asher tried but failed to suppress a laugh.

Reuben turned cold, annoyed eyes on him, then back to me. "Then why are you here?"

I lowered my arms to my sides and curled my hands into fists. Turns out, the urge to punch him wasn't just initial. I still had it.

"I'm here to tell you to stay the fuck away from Abbie. In fact, you'd be better off staying the fuck away from me and anyone associated with me."

He looked unimpressed, maybe even amused. He was certainly not intimidated. I didn't expect him to be. Fuckers like him weren't easily scared. Shame, I wouldn't mind seeing some fear in his eyes once in a while.

"I'm happy to stay away from her," he said slowly. "You know what you need to do to make that happen." He spoke in an even, reasonable tone, like he was talking to a kid who didn't fully grasp the situation.

"Yes, I do." I pretended to misunderstand. "I'd prefer not to kill you, though. I don't enjoy having blood on my hands as much as you do." Although, I might make an exception if it was his. That would solve a bunch of my problems. And create new ones. My brothers would be pissed if I did it. Except Caleb, who might be happy to take his place as head of the family. Maybe I could cut a deal with him...

"Liar," Reuben scoffed. "You can deny it all you want, but it's who you are, just like it's who I am. Just like it's who he is." He inclined his head slightly in Asher's direction.

"I can find a place in the organisation for him too. And Abbie, if you insist. She has the same undercurrent of barely suppressed violence the rest of us do."

"If by that you mean she wanted to kick you in the balls, yes, she does," I agreed. "She doesn't want to join the organisation any more than I do. Neither does Asher."

"Nope, Asher doesn't," he said without glancing up from his book. "I'll leave that bullshit to Dane. Anyone else with the last name DiMarco wants to stay right out of it."

Reuben's eyes flicked towards Asher and something crossed his features. It was so brief I almost missed it. What was that about? Annoyance at Asher's declaration that he wouldn't be coming back to the fold either?

I didn't think that was it. Reuben had never cared what Asher thought before, why would he now?

Unless… Unless he thought Asher was the reason for my refusal. He was certainly a part of it. Still, I sensed something else was going on in my brother's head. Whatever it was, I was better off not trying to figure it out.

I sucked in an irritated breath.

"Would it help if I took out a sky writer?" I asked. "In the sky they could write in big, fat letters, 'I'm not coming back.' Would you get it then?"

I suspected he wouldn't get it if I wrote it on the wall with his blood. The fact that was tempting suggested maybe he had a point about the violence of this life being a part of me. Or maybe I was just fed up with his bullshit.

"You can't sing without a tongue," Reuben said simply. "And you can't have a band without the band."

"Don't threaten me," I growled.

He scoffed. "You know me better than that. I don't make threats. If you don't obey, and soon, I will make all of these things happen. You know I can and will."

"You're a motherfucker," I said coldly enough to match his tone. "You have enough people working for you. You don't need me. I'm not going to go around killing for you, so I'd be no use to you anyway."

"You would be useful in a hundred different ways," Reuben said. "Is that what you're concerned about? That you'll have nothing to do but sit around in my library and admire my books?"

"They are pretty awesome books," Asher said helpfully. "Especially this one." He held it up.

"No, I'm not worried about being bored," I said. "Or having nothing else to do but read."

Hell, that sounded enticing. Would he pay me to sit in his library and read his books? I might actually consider it if that was what was on the table.

Fuck, what was I thinking? There was no way that was all there was to this. Even if it was, I didn't want to give up my life to him.

Besides, I had enough money that I could spend the rest of my life sitting around reading if I wanted to. I didn't need Reuben's help with that.

"I love my life," I said with finality. "I don't want to stop doing what I'm doing. I don't want to work for you. I want you to stay the hell out of my life. And away from me, Abbie and the band. How can I possibly make that any clearer? Do I need to get 'stay the fuck away from me' tattooed on my forehead?"

"Can I dare you to do that?" Asher looked up from his book and grinned.

"Let's put that on the maybe pile," I told him. "At this point it's a second last resort." I'd do it if it would actually work.

On the other hand, it might send the wrong message to fans of the band. That would suck. Maybe I could get it tattooed inside my lower lip so I could pull it out and show him whenever he pissed me off. That would work for a lot of people too, not just Reuben.

"The last resort being killing me," Reuben said dryly.

"Yeah, but that's quickly moving its way up the

list." I narrowed my eyes at him. If he thought I was joking, he would have to think again. I didn't want to kill him, but we couldn't keep having this argument over and over again. And I couldn't let him kill people I loved so I'd obey him.

Reuben sighed dramatically. "You repeatedly say this life isn't for you, but then you make threats like that, proving yourself wrong. Sooner or later you will come to accept that. Sooner would be better for everyone, particularly you."

I responded with an exasperated growl from deep in the back of my throat.

"Being stubborn is a great personality trait to have, but you have to know when to give up. Because I'm not going to." I can't believe I actually considered it.

Maybe if he wasn't such an asshole, I would have agreed to give up the band eventually. Since he was a world class motherfucking prick, I was more determined than ever to stick to my guns. So to speak.

Reuben looked absolutely unmoved and undeterred. "You will. Is there anything else you want? If not, I have...things to get back to."

His pause was barely perceptible, but it was there.

Things? What was I missing here? Would he even

MAGGIE ALABASTER & JO BRADLEY

tell me if I asked? Probably not. If he did, there would be strings attached to the response. It was probably better I didn't know.

He might have someone down in the basement he was in the middle of torturing or killing. It wouldn't surprise me one bit. I even listened for screams, but didn't hear any.

What was I thinking? His basement, if he had one, it would be soundproofed. He was a dickhead, but he wasn't stupid.

"Don't let me keep you," I said coolly. "I also have things to do. Like celebrating the fact our latest song reached number one on the charts. But you wouldn't care about that, would you?" I crossed my arms and smirked.

"Not in the slightest," he agreed. If anything, he looked mildly disgusted.

At least one of us was happy for me and the guys.

"And you wonder why I don't want to come back," I said sarcastically. "Did it ever occur to you to offer your little brother some support? Maybe if you took an interest in the things I like, I would take an interest in yours." That was highly unlikely and we all knew it.

"When you do something interesting, I'll be interested," he said. "Anyone can shout into a microphone."

"That's true," I agreed. "It's much harder to *sing* into one. You should try it sometime, it's therapeutic." According to my father, Reuben was in the boys' choir before I was born.

By the sound of it, he had an amazing voice until it broke. Maybe that was why he hated what I did so much. Because he didn't get to do it himself. Honestly, that was one hundred percent his problem, not mine.

"I would pay to see that duet," Asher said. "Reuben could give up a life of crime and join the band."

We both turned and looked at him.

He shrugged. "Or maybe not."

"There's only room for one Brantley in Wolf Venom," I said. "And it's not Reuben."

Although, let's face it, if it got him off my back about working for him, I'd actually consider it. He could be a backing singer, or maybe a roadie.

As if any of that would happen.

Honestly, it would be better if it didn't. I didn't want my brother anywhere near Abbie or the other guys. Or me.

I had to figure out a way to get him to listen.

Preferably one that didn't involve bloodshed. I wished I had a clue what it would take to get him to back off once and for all. Whatever it was, I'd do it.

I had a sinking feeling he wouldn't give up until I was dead, or he was.

24

ABBIE

"I bet you were amazing." Tully was beside me the moment I stepped out of the studio.

Landon wasn't too far behind him. For once, he wasn't in Channing's company. Everyone needed some time apart once in a while, I supposed.

Penn was nowhere to be seen. That wasn't surprising. Unless it was directly related to the band, he was usually not around. If he was, he was busy scowling and making snide remarks.

"I hope so," I said. "It felt good. Candy seemed happy. She's so great to work with."

"She is," Tully agreed. He slipped his hand into one of mine. "She's the best in the business. I think she might be a magician. After all, she makes us sound good." He grinned.

"Hey." Landon slid over to walk on the other side of me. "*We* make us sound good. She makes us sound incredible."

"Close enough," Tully said. "Zeke suggested we might walk you home and stay with you for a while."

"He and Asher aren't back yet?" I asked. I had no idea where they went, just that they had something they had to take care of. I had a feeling it involved Reuben, but I hadn't asked. When it came to him, it was probably better I didn't know. What is it they say? Ignorance is bliss.

"Not yet," Tully said lightly.

I had the distinct impression he knew exactly what was going on. He didn't seem too worried, so I would follow his lead and not be concerned. Well, not be more concerned than I already was.

I'd feel better when both guys were back from whatever it was they were doing. Hopefully it didn't involve anything illegal. And if it did, hopefully they didn't get caught. I trusted them both enough to know if they did something, they did it for good reason.

Should I be so accepting of them possibly doing something against the law? No, but it was still kinda hot. Yeah, I'm a flawed human, sue me. I felt safer with them than I ever had with anyone else. And a lot more turned on.

I turned to Landon. "Where's Channing?"

He shrugged and responded with the same light tone as Tully. "He has some stuff to take care of. It shouldn't take long, then we should all go to the pub. We have a song to celebrate."

I smiled. "I'm so proud of you guys. I'm not even slightly surprised everyone loves it as much as they do. And the whole album. It's definitely your best yet." It really was. I wouldn't have thought they could top the last one, but they had. The sound was both very them and fresh at the same time. The emotion in the lyrics, the way the instruments played off each other, the...

I could rave about it for days. Honestly, I already had.

"Hell yeah it is." Landon grinned. He was only a year or two younger than me, but he seemed so untouched by the bad in the world. It wasn't that he was innocent, just that he wasn't jaded. Compared to me, anyway. I was jaded enough for all of us.

Either way, his enthusiasm and joy for life was endearing and adorable. And his hair was such a great shade of blue. It brought out the blue in his hazel eyes, and made his tanned skin look a shade or two darker.

He had two full sleeves of tattoos, and muscles ready to burst out of the sleeves of his dark grey tee. He wore a couple of chains around his neck and a ring on his right thumb. A leather bracelet on his right wrist completed the whole rock star look.

He probably had men and women following him around everywhere.

"Yours will be too," he added. "You have a much better label now, and better support to make it exactly what you want it to be." He spoke with such confidence and sincerity, he obviously adored White Wolf Records. That confidence was infectious too.

"You know what, you're right," I said. "I have maturity and I have all of those things as well. There's no reason I can't go platinum this time."

"Multi-platinum," Tully said. "This time next year, you'll be headlining the tour and we'll be supporting you."

I let out a choking laugh. "Wolf Venom will never be supporting me. You guys are so big you'll never support anyone. Not on tour anyway."

"At least we can support you in every other way that counts," Landon said. "Can we have front row tickets when you headline?" He actually looked hopeful, as if there was a chance I'd say no.

"Absolutely. Front row, backstage, whatever you want," I said. "As long as you're there, cheering me on."

Knowing my luck, we'd both end up on tour at the same time, but travelling to different cities on opposite sides of the planet. That might be unavoidable, but it was also something I would worry about if it happened.

"We wouldn't be anywhere else," Tully said assuringly. He squeezed my hand gently, then started to trace circles over my skin with his thumb.

Should it feel strange to touch him like this after being so close to Zeke and Asher? Possibly, but it didn't. Everything about spending time with all the guys felt right.

I looked over at him and smiled. Then looked over to Landon and did the same.

Landon grinned back and took my other hand in his.

We walked past a couple of the people who worked for the label. They gave us some raised eyebrows, but that was all. It was incredibly gratifying not to feel judged by these people who invested so much in me already.

At some point, I was going to wake up from this and realise it was all a beautiful dream. If that was the case, then I hoped I would sleep for a hundred years. Or two hundred. Or forever.

There probably weren't any spinning wheels in the building, but they might be a turntable with a needle I could prick my finger on. That might ensure I stayed asleep for long enough to make this fairytale last.

We stepped out of the building into the sunshine of the late afternoon. I blinked my eyes against the sudden glare. I hadn't realised quite how long I spent in the studio until now. No regrets, but the sudden burst of daylight was jarring.

"Hey." Channing trotted over to us from the direction of the car park. He glanced at the way Landon held my hand and smiled.

When I thought Landon might let go, he didn't. He gave Channing a quick kiss when he got close enough, but kept holding on to me.

"Did you get things sorted out?" Landon asked him.

"Yep," Channing said lightly. "All good."

"Is everything all right?" I realised how little I knew about him and Landon. They might be into the same things as Zeke and Asher's families were, for all I knew. Or worse.

They looked more innocent than the other guys, but then again, so did Parker and Hunter Brantley.

Looking innocent was no real indication of actual innocence. My reflection was proof of that.

I still trusted them as much as I trusted the other guys.

"Everything is perfect," Channing said. "Just tying up some loose ends before we go on tour."

Those words sent a ripple of excitement through me. There was nothing I loved more than singing in front of a live crowd. That was why we did this. Seeing the excited faces, listening to people singing your words back to you, watching them dance to your music, knowing they'd waited anywhere up to a year for this one night.

It was everything. The biggest rush there was.

I nodded. "Great. It's good to be organised."

"Were you worried about me?" He grinned.

"There's someone running around who cut off a man's head and left it in a cardboard box," I reminded him. "Not to mention Zeke's brother, who seemed to think it was okay to abduct me off the side of the street. Of course I was worried. I'm always going to worry while one of you is off by yourself."

"That's so sweet." Channing stepped around in front of me so I had to stop walking. He cupped my cheeks with his hands and kissed my mouth. "You're so sweet."

I found myself kissing him back and there was nothing even slightly strange about doing it. Not even when Tully held one of my hands and Landon held the other.

By the time we broke apart, I was breathless, and all three of the guys were grinning. I could get used to this, being the centre of attention for all of these gorgeous men.

If they weren't careful, I might start to feel like a queen. They all made me feel more special than anyone else ever had. Individually, they were amazing. Collectively, they were mind blowing.

Before I could gather my thoughts again, Landon turned my face toward his and he kissed me too, as deep and full as Channing had.

"Definitely sweet," he said, his lips still on mine.

We barely broke apart before Tully turned my face toward his and kissed me with lips and tongue and teeth.

All of this attention was turning my knees to

jelly. If we kept doing this, someone was going to have to carry me to Zeke's place. My legs would give out before too much longer.

"We should get you home," Tully said reluctantly.

"Yeah." That was probably better than fucking out here in the street, up against a car, in broad daylight, because that was where this would end up if we weren't careful.

Okay, I wouldn't be mad about that. Until a paparazzi spotted us and took photos. Fucking clit blockers.

"Come on then," Landon said. He tugged me forward with our joined hands and we all resumed walking.

"Do any of you know what Zeke and Asher were up to?" I asked reluctantly.

They all exchanged looks which gave me my answer. They knew exactly what the other guys were doing. Judging by the way they all pressed their lips together, they weren't going to tell me. Each was a brick wall of silence.

"Should I be concerned about them?" I asked. I sighed. "Of course I should. Please tell me they didn't do something stupid."

"That depends on your definition of stupid," Landon said.

"Anything which would get them killed," I said. "Or arrested. Or if they had to visit Haru to dispose of evidence. Or anything that would make the label drop them. Or anything that involves buying too many canned goods."

Okay, I don't know why my mind went there, except that it was difficult to store too many cans and Zeke's townhouse was small.

"I can one hundred percent guarantee you they are not buying too many canned goods," Tully said.

I waited.

"You can't guarantee anything else, can you?" I groaned.

No one answered.

I shook my head. Apparently all I could do was hope they turned up in one piece before too much longer. I wouldn't relax until I saw them both with my own two eyes.

"They'll be fine," Tully assured me. "They can take care of themselves."

"I hope so," I said. I fell into a worried silence while we walked, thoughts of fucking gone for now.

They were pushed further away at the sound of excited voices a block from Zeke's townhouse.

At first, I assumed it had something to do with him and Asher.

Until we rounded the corner and saw the throng of press outside his house.

"There she is," one of them shouted.

Like a swarm of ants, journalists with their microphones and cameras, or phones, in their hands started toward us.

Specifically, towards me.

I let go of the guys' hands to keep them from falling under any scrutiny. I immediately wished I hadn't, because their touch was comforting. Without it, I felt naked.

"Abbie Hart, do you have any comments to make?" A microphone was shoved in my face.

I frowned at the man who held it. "About what?" Oh God, what had happened to Zeke and Asher? My heart raced and panic started to rise.

"About the death of Vance," the journalist said.

I blinked. "I beg your pardon?" Was I hearing right?

"You didn't know?" Did he have to look so happy about breaking news like that to me? I must look like a deer in headlights.

"No." I shook my head. "That's terrible." Ish. "I'm so sorry for what his family must be going through."

"I'm sure you would agree it's particularly hard

on his fiancée who found him. Or the one part of him," the journalist said.

"The one..." Oh God, please tell me this wasn't what I thought it was.

"Yes. Evidently she found his head on her front doorstep in a cardboard box."

The whole world started to spin.

ABOUT THE AUTHOR

Maggie Alabaster writes reverse harem and, paranormal, sci-fi and fantasy romance.

She lives in NSW, Australia with one spouse, two daughters, one dog, and countless birds.

Jo Bradley is her alternate personality. She writes contemporary romance.

Sign up for my newsletter! Sign Up!

Join my reader group! Join here!

Follow me on Bookbub! Click here to follow me!

Check out my website- www.maggiealabaster.com

ALSO BY MAGGIE ALABASTER

Saving Abbie

Book 1 Pitch

Book 2 Pound

Book 3 Session

Book 4 Muse

Book 5 Rhythm

Book 6 Encore

Ruthless Claws

Book 1 Ivory

Book 2 Crimson

Book 3 Elodie

Harmony's Magic

Book 1 Summoned by Fire

Book 2 Summoned by Fate

Book 3 Summoned by Desire

Shifter's Vault

Book 1 Discarded

Also by Maggie Alabaster and Erin Yoshikawa

Caught by the Tide